FIRST FICT

INTRODUCTION

A. O. Chater
Alan Coren
Ted Hughes
Jim Hunter
Jason McManus
Julian Mitchell

INTRODUCTION 2

Francis Hope
Sheila Macleod
Angus Stewart
Tom Stoppard
Garth St Omer

INTRODUCTION 3

Rachel Bush
Christopher Hampton
Michael Hoyland
Roy Watkins
John Wheway

INTRODUCTION 4

Ian Cochrane
Vincent Lawrence
Brian Phelan
Neil Rathmell
Irene Summy

INTRODUCTION 5

Adrian Kenny
Sara Maitland
David Pownall
Alice Rowe
Lorna Tracy

INTRODUCTION 6

John Abulafia
Jim Crace
Thomas Healy
Victor Kelleher
John Mackendrick

INTRODUCTION 7

Kazuo Ishiguro
J. K. Klavans
Steven Kupfer
Tim Owens
Amanda Hemingway

INTRODUCTION 8

Anne Devlin
Ronald Frame
Helen Harris
Rachel Gould
Robert Sproat

INTRODUCTION 9

Douglas Glover
Kristien Hemmerechts
Deirdre Madden
Deborah Moffatt
Dorothy Nimmo
Jaci Stephen

FIRST FICTIONS 10

An Introduction

'This venture is the best of its kind.'
Sunday Times

faber and faber
LONDON · BOSTON

First published in 1989 by
Faber and Faber Limited
3 Queen Square London WC1N 3AU

Photoset by Wilmaset Birkenhead Wirral
Printed in Great Britain by
Richard Clay Ltd Bungay Suffolk

All rights reserved

This anthology © Faber and Faber Limited, 1989

*This book is sold subject to the condition that it shall not,
by way of trade or otherwise, be lent, resold, hired out
or otherwise circulated without the publisher's prior consent
in any form of binding or cover other than that in which
it is published and without a similar condition including this
condition being imposed on the subsequent purchaser.*

British Library Cataloguing in Publication Data is available.

ISBN 0–571–15201–5

CONTENTS

	page
CAROLE MORIN	
Thin White Girls	3
The Hotel Summer	16
Practically Park Lane	27
MATTHEW FRANCIS	
Green Winter	35
Demonland	44
American Fugue	52
KATHY O'SHAUGHNESSY	
On the Threshold	65
The Story	73
A Problematic Tale	78
A Rainy Day	89
TOM HARPOLE	
The Last of Butch	95
Making a Moose Die	110
ANNE ENRIGHT	
Smile	121
Felix	124
Thirst	136
Seascape	141

CONTENTS

HUGO HAMILTON

The Supremacy of Grief	151
The Compound Assembly of E. Richter	158
Above and Beyond	174

Publisher's Note

In this collection, the tenth to appear in the prose INTRODUCTION series, it is our aim once again to bring new writers to the attention of a wider reading public. None of the contributors has had work published in book form before. As always, the number of writers is restricted to give each the advantage of presenting a substantial amount of work.

The INTRODUCTION series has seen the first publication of several successful authors. They include Ted Hughes, Julian Mitchell, Tom Stoppard, Christopher Hampton, Kazuo Ishiguro, Anne Devlin and Deirdre Madden.

Biographical Notes

Carole Morin was born in 1964, in Glasgow. She currently lives in London.

Matthew Francis was born in Hampshire in 1956. He studied English at Cambridge and American Literature at the University of Sussex. He now works as a freelance author of computer manuals. He writes poetry as well as fiction, and has won several prizes, notably in the National Poetry Competition. *Green Winter* was first published in *Encounter*.

Kathy O'Shaughnessy grew up in North London. She gained a first-class degree in English at Oxford University, and then spent a year doing an M.Phil. on Byron. She left that to become deputy editor on the *Literary Review*. She is currently Arts Editor on *Vogue*. She is twenty-nine.

Tom Harpole was born in 1949 in Deer Lodge, Montana. He worked as a logger, carpenter, miner and blaster until a logging accident ended his manual labours. He is an American/Irish dual national and he and his wife divide their time between Montana and Ireland. He studied creative writing at the University College of Galway and Carroll College of Montana. He has been published in several literary journals in Ireland and America.

BIOGRAPHICAL NOTES

Anne Enright was born in 1962. She attended Trinity College, Dublin, and, with the aid of a British Council Grant, took an MA in Creative Writing in Norwich, taught by Malcolm Bradbury and Angela Carter. She has worked with fringe theatres in Dublin and is now a television producer in Ireland. She started writing prose in 1986. Special thanks to Bernard and Mary Loughlin of the Tyrone Guthrie Centre, Annaghmakerrig.

Hugo Hamilton was born in Dublin in 1953. His father was Irish and his mother German. He became involved in journalism and lived in Germany and Austria during the late seventies. He returned to Dublin where he now lives and has been working for some time in the recording business and in publishing. More recently, he has been engaged in full-time writing and has had stories published in *New Irish Writing* and the *Irish Times*. His story 'The Supremacy of Grief' was first published in *New Irish Writing* (*The Irish Press*), November 1986.

CAROLE MORIN

Thin White Girls

One day last summer, when I was ugly and unhappy, I got out a terrible photograph of me that Dad had taken – before he went funny – and ripped it up. I enjoyed shredding it with my fingers, then cut it with Mum's sharpest scissors I had to look for ages in the work basket for. I thought then that I may be a psycho. But Jack says you aren't, if you think it. The ones who think it never are. It's like thinking you're going to be murdered, then you aren't. I used to think I was the only one who thought that, but my brother Danny told me that everyone does. He says it's because people can't accept that they're just going to die like everyone else, just a normal death with a funeral and nothing in the newspapers, unless it's the memorial column. But Jack says you don't have to die. He doesn't intend to. He says it's silly to assume that you will, just because everybody else does. I said I'd like to die, instead of being all wrinkled and ugly. But Danny laughed at me again and said everyone thinks that as well. At ten you think you want to die when you're twenty-one, then when you're that age you think: 'I'll do it when I'm thirty'. But instead you keep on living like everyone else – until something happens. I said I don't care what everyone else does, I want to die when I'm still young – after I'm rich and have done everything so there's no point in going on. But Jack was adamant. 'I'm not going to die,' he said. 'I'm going to wait and see what happens.'

My mum says Jack's crazy and she doesn't want me hanging round with him as much, but Danny says she can't stop me.

'Not unless she locks me in,' I said. Kids in books get locked in all the time.

'There ain't no locks on our doors, dummy,' Danny said.
'Oh yeah,' I said.
We talk about getting old a lot. That, and fat people. I think about toilets a lot, and how awful it must be to *be* a toilet. Once, in room three, I wrote a story about a toilet. It was one of those stories when it's about the person writing it, so everything's 'I', except the 'I' hasn't to be yourself, if you see what I mean. I decided to be a toilet, and took ages writing it. But Miss Scone was mad as shit and kept me behind after school and told me not to do anything like that again. So I haven't. When we're told to be someone else now I write about Crispin Glover and Colonel H like the other kids. But really I know my idea was much better, and when I'm out of her school I'll write about toilets as much as I like.

I think about kissing a lot too. It's such a revolting thing to do. You have to get close to the person, and touch them, and touch their slevvers with your mouth. I'd hate to do it, but one day I suppose I'll have to or I'll be queer. People in Danny's class go to clubs and 'get off with people'. The more the better, they seem to think. I've even heard Danny say it can cause a *disease*. I can't imagine myself ever being able to do anything like that, or Jack for that matter. But I suppose I will. Just like growing old. Jack says growing old isn't as bad as you think. He says when you see yourself in a picture or something you'll feel the same as you do when you look at a baby picture now. And you'll get old so slowly that you won't even notice. 'It's happening now,' he said.

I'm not sure if I believe him, about not noticing. I think I will definitely notice. I've seen a few wrinkles already. They're worse when it's sunny. I hate the sun, it's so boring. Everyone thinks it's such a big deal getting a tan, but they hate Puerto Ricans and Jungle Bunnies and people like that. I don't ever want a sun-tan. I'll be a thin white girl for ever.

I had a dream last night that I was in New York, crossing some real busy street like Fifth Avenue or somewhere, and this black guy tried to mug me. I remember thinking, right there in the dream, that it was pretty stupid in the middle of the road, because we both could've been knocked down. Anyway, his name turned out to be Adam, so I called him Black Adam, and we got on pretty well so he decided not to mug me after all. I'd tell you more about it, 'cos it was quite long, but Jack says it's always real boring when somebody tells you about their dream, people only like their own dreams. Jack says he dreams about murder a lot, and I said I do too. I'm always being murdered, or just about, but he dreams he is murdering people.

Day-dreams are terrible things. Always based on hope. Hope is a terrible thing, unless it's something to do with money. Money's the only thing that doesn't disappoint you. Everything else that you hope for either doesn't happen or when it does it's not been worth the wait. Even if money doesn't happen it's still worth hoping for. It's always worth having. It doesn't let you down. You can do just about anything with it. People say that money doesn't buy you health, but Jack says it can. It buys you hospitals and specialists and new blood and research teams anyway. People like my mum and ministers say it doesn't buy you happiness, and our teacher last year made us all put up our hands if we'd like to be rich, and keep our hands up if we'd like money at the expense of our happiness. I put mine down, because I knew that's what she wanted, but I hate her now. I mean, poverty doesn't buy you happiness either. What chance has it got if money doesn't work? Money *is* happiness to some people and I expect I'm one of them. I'm sure Jack is too. My brother Danny doesn't believe in money – so he says – but he still needs it when he's going out. He gets it from my mum. I get money from her when I'm going out too, or for the ice-cream van, but I don't need it. I've got some of my own.

I'm always talking to myself. It's been happening for years and I never gave it a second thought. Until recently, when I started doing it outside and in front of people without noticing. Only once or twice. But still, it can't be normal. I asked Jack and he said he never talks to himself. That can't be normal either. 'I can stop anytime I want to,' I said when we were on the bus to the graveyard. We'd never been that far before alone.

But I tried it, and it wasn't that easy. Instead of saying the words out loud, I just started saying them into myself – moving my lips without much sound coming out like David Byrne's imitation of a preacher. I'm still sure I could stop completely, if it was really necessary.

The bus was pretty full, and there were even dogs on it. Jack hates dogs, and says he'd like to go out one night in the dark and shoot them all. I said, 'You haven't got a gun,' and he smiled at me and said nothing. I love it when he does that. It reminds me of the movies. Jack loves night-time, and Dracula, and says when he's older he's never gonna get up during the day. He'll live in a darkened room, or a cellar, and only go out at night. When there's nobody about. Well, only interesting people, and interesting things going on.

The gardens were full, outside on the lawns, but the mausoleums were empty 'cos it was too cool for everyone in there. A girl was sitting on the grass in a bikini that was too small for her, and there was a man with a fat stomach lying next to her. He wasn't that fat anywhere else, just his gruesome big stomach.

We went inside and looked at the tombs for a while without saying much. Then we wandered around in the park, away from the lawns where there's a river and a bridge and a really steep set of stairs leading down to the river's edge, with no people about. We climbed down, glaring at everyone who passed on their way up to the sun.

'We won't get the bus back,' Jack said. 'We'll walk.'

He hates buses 'cos they're full of germs and fat people. The worst thing of all is when a fat person sits next to you, squashing you into the window, and you can hardly breathe, and you end up getting off before your stop it's so awful.

'Yes, OK,' I said, though my mum would be mad if I was late for my tea. She doesn't like me going far. Especially not with Jack. She says he's 'far too adventurous for a seven-year-old'.

On the way out of the graveyard we saw a sign saying they close at ten.

'I'd love to be in here when it shuts,' he said. 'Hiding behind the stones.'

'Yeah,' I said.

My feet were all blistered when I got home.

'Your dinner's ruined,' Mum said. She said she was keeping me in as well, but didn't. She must've forgot. Danny said she didn't forget, she just changed her mind. But I still think she forgot. 'When I make my mind up I stick to it.' I've heard her say that often enough.

The graveyard was pretty busy next day, with men cutting grass and straightening stones. No one was being dug in. Nobody has for ages. Danny says there's probably no room left, but my mum thinks it's because people are being cremated these days. She says that's more hygenic than having a load of insects eating away at you. I said I wanted her ashes, and Danny said he'd get them 'cos he's older, and I started to cry. Mum said they'd be left in the Hall of Remembrance anyway. But I said, 'If somebody gets to keep them, will it be me?' and she smiled, so he started up, and she decided we could halve them.

It was hot in the park again, and everyone was sneezing germs over everyone else. I hate that. We climbed under the bushes, practising. Jack says when he gets enough money he wants to go to New York and hide in the bushes in Central Park. He'll go wearing good clothes, and only stay for about three days. He won't need a hotel or anything, 'cos he'll be in the bushes at night, and just hanging out during the day. I'd like to go as well, but not with him. It's best to go alone.

In the afternoon there was a thunderstorm so we went into Jack's house and watched TV with the sound down. His mum was doing washing in the kitchen the whole time and only popped in twice. Once to give us Irn Bru and biscuits, and once to see why the TV was so quiet. Jack said, 'The sound's down,' and Mrs Revola said, 'Oh,' then went back to her kitchen. If that had been my mother there would've been twenty questions. She'd have wanted an explanation and would probably have made us change the channel as well for no good reason.

The storm made it real warm. 'Clammy' I think it's called, but that's one of those words I hate. I just die when people use an embarrassing word like that. There are others that are worse; but I can't bear to say any of them. To even think them. Jack says there's something dirty about heat, and something clean about the cold. I can't explain it, but know what he means. I love looking at ice, or clean snow. I could almost eat it sometimes it's so fresh and chill. I love sucking ice cubes from the fridge, though Danny usually tells on me and I get slapped in case I end up with worms. But the heat makes you all dirty and sticky, and the sun makes you tired. It gives me migraine as well. And lots of fat people are about, revolting everyone with their flab and tight clothes. I could just die when it's sunny sometimes, though it's better weather for staying out all night. I'd just die if I was fat. I'm determined. (All my teachers say that.) I'll be a thin white girl for ever.

'Thin white girls come out in the dark and eat babies.' They don't really but my brother Danny says things like that. All the time. It's supposed to annoy me, but it doesn't. Danny's silly. He says that I won't really be rich when I grow up, and neither will Jack. He says everyone thinks that at our age, 'cos they can't stand the thought of being mediocre. But that they grow out of it. He seems to think that just 'cos he's older that means he knows much more than us. My dad's like that as well. I'm sure it's not true. Not always. I mean, a young smart person is much better than an old stupid one. But I suppose maybe an old smart one could have the advantage on a young smart one. But they wouldn't be able to run as fast. I'm sure there's nothing as good as being young. My dad says I should keep my ideas to myself, until I know what I'm talking about. He's a lot older and a lot wiser than I'll ever be. I said, 'But, Dad, Mrs Thatcher's older than you – she must be with all those veins. Does that mean she's wiser?' That shut him up.

Danny said I'm a liar as well as being stupid, and Mum slapped him and told him not to swear then she slapped me and told me not to smirk. She asked, 'Whatever made you say a thing like that about your little sister?' And Danny said, "Cos she is.' And Mummy asked why and he said, blushing, "Cos she said she never shits, and that can't be true 'cos everybody does.' She smacked him again for saying a bad word, and then me too. I asked how come and she said I must've said the bad word as well when she wasn't there, and I screamed: 'No, I never did, I said jobbie. And it's true, I never . . .' After that she interrupted and said, 'That was the end of it,' and I was going to my bed if I didn't behave. I figured that I'd be going anyway, but shut up just in case. There might be something on TV I wanted to see later. But I hate Danny sometimes. I wish Jack was my brother. Or Danny was more like Alan. And it's true. I don't shit. It's too dirty for me.

We got *Wuthering Heights* in school for our new reader. I saw it on TV and thought it was great, but hate it now. Mr Wills said we'd make it into a sort of play, and different people would get turns at reading parts aloud. That sounded OK at first, but he takes all the good bits for himself. And I mean, it's our reader. I wanted to be Heathcliff, 'cos he's the best, but I'm a girl so he wouldn't let me. But I bet he wouldn't have let me even if I was a boy 'cos he could've picked Jack or somebody for the part. But he didn't. He took it for himself. And I mean, it's us that's meant to be practising our reading. I told my mum at teatime, and I said I'd get my own back. Later on I'm going to be an actor, and be Heathcliff and all the good parts. But Danny laughed and said I couldn't be, and I said, 'I'll get my hair cut short and they won't know,' and he said, 'You still can't be an actress, you hate putting other people's clothes on.' That's true. I won't have anything to do with hand-me-downs. I never touch them, never mind put them on – no matter how much Mum coaxes or what story she concocts about where they came from. I just wouldn't be seen dead in somebody else's skirt. Jack says it's one of the quickest ways to catch something and he should know. His dad died of cancer a few years ago. But Jack says too that there's a lot of actors who are really men, dressed up as women, so women can probably dress as men as well. He should know, he's seen them. Some of them aren't even actors either. I bet there's a lot of them going around just now, men like Nic Cage and Arnold Schwarzenegger and Vincent d'Onofrio – when really they're women. I'm not that easily fooled. Of course, I don't want to actually be a man. Just Heathcliff. I like being a girl. Thin white girls are best of all.

Danny went on Scout Camp Week. My dad's a leader (at least he was, until he went funny) and Mum goes up with them as well for the day to help get things started. She drives one of the minibuses too. At one point it looked as if I might have to go as well – just for the day – and I would've missed going to the movies with Jack in the afternoon. But, at the last minute, my other brother Alan (who's much older than me and Danny and has a different mother) came back unexpectedly. Him and his friend. So I was allowed to stay, if I was good. I said I would be, for definite, and Alan said he didn't mind. He'd watch me in the morning until Mrs Revola picked me up, and Mrs Revola said I could go to her house for my tea. I was pleased. I get along with Alan OK – he's not a nuisance like Danny – and I like having my tea at Jack's house. We always get good stuff to eat, and I can clean my teeth to death without Mum complaining that I'll brush them away.

Alan and his friend stayed in his room. I watched the *Saturday Show* then got pretty bored with the cartoons that are on after. I hate cartoons, they're so silly. I went along to Alan's room, and they were sitting on the floor smoking. 'You haven't unpacked yet,' I said, just for something to say. They just smiled. 'How long you staying?' I asked.

'I don't know,' Alan said, after quite a long pause. I was going to ask where they'd been, but could tell they didn't feel like talking to me. Not that they were rude or anything, I could just tell.

'See ya,' I said, and went along to my own room for a bit. I decided to wait in the garden, and see how many wasps I could spot before Jack came. He counted three hundred and sixty-seven one day waiting for me. I looked through the crack in Alan's door as I passed, a habit I have. It isn't really spying, just something I always do whether there's anyone in the room or not. Alan's friend was squeezing his hand, clenching the fist right in, then letting it out, with Alan's old Stonewall tie around his arm. I thought that looked pretty funny, and was about to go in and see what they were up to when I saw Alan's hand through the crack as well. It was holding a needle. And he stuck it into his friend's arm. That happened to me once.

I didn't make a noise. I knew if they saw me, they'd make me go away. Not that I wanted to go in there with them. I hate needles, and was glad I couldn't see the look on his friend's face. A few minutes later, the needle switched hands. I knew it was Alan's turn, and didn't stay to watch this time. I ran outside and started counting.

When Mrs Revola tooted I was at thirty-one. Alan came to the door and waved us off. I didn't tell Jack about what I'd seen until after the film. 'I've heard of that,' he said. 'It must be what people mean when they talk about getting a real shot in the arm.'

My friend Eileen and I ate shit.

When we got back to school nobody believed us. Jack and I don't always hang around together in school. We go together in the morning, and get each other home later, but he's in the boys' playground and I'm in the other one. We have different lunch times as well – we have to go half an hour earlier. I have five best friends out of the girls in my class. There's Eileen, Linda, Lisa, Jannie and Elize. Miss Allison calls us Soph's Club 'cos we always go everywhere together and I'm sort of the leader. Jack has a bunch of friends as well. Everyone likes him. (Except my mum, but she doesn't know anything.)

After lunch, we have places we always go. Like the arcade, or the embankment down at the back of the employment exchange beside the railway, or the swings, or just back to the playground. One day in the arcade car-park we were playing hide and seek from the watchie who always chases us out of there. Eileen and I were behind this big lorry. We were there for ages without getting caught, and it got pretty boring so we started chalking our names on the side, then writing other things when we got fed up with that. Then Jannie shouted that it was time to go back, and we all ran down to the school in time for the bell. But our hands – Eileen's and mine – were filthy from the lorry. A hard, brown, chalk crust was stuck to them, and at the same time, for no reason, we just licked them. So it's not as bad as it sounds. We didn't mean to eat shit. How were we to know that's what was on the lorry?

'You might've *smelled* it,' Jack said, on our way home.

'Well . . .' I said, 'the car-park smells anyway.'

And that's true. A lot of dogs go up there to shit.

Next morning they were all still talking about it. Sandra James asked Miss Allison if Eileen and me would die. And Roger Royson – a boy in Jack's group that I hate – said how did we know it was shit, unless we're really filthy and eat it all the time and know *exactly* what it tastes like. Miss Allison said that was enough, and she didn't want any of us going near the car-park again. We never have, just in case. I mean, jobbies are just germs, aren't they? And you're best keeping away from them, if you want a happy life.

But I know that it was shit. And I'm glad I ate it – even if it was a mistake at the time. I mean, it's an experience. And one not many people have. How many people do you know who can say 'I've eaten shit' and be telling the truth? Months later, down the swing park one Sunday afternoon, Jack said: 'I wish I'd been there.' I was about to ask where, but stopped. I know what he meant.

Thin white girls don't cry. Thin white girls live for ever. I'm a thin white girl, I'll live longer.

Alan didn't used to be as bad. He's always been quiet, but is really cute and wears nice shirts and Danny says 'girls are after him'. But then he hardly went out, just sat in his room with some of his friends and they would all leave when my mum got in. I heard Mum say to Dad that 'it would have to stop' and 'she wasn't having it go on in her house' and he'd 'have to give him a talking to, he's his son'. But I don't think they were all that bad. I mean, they didn't make that much noise – not like me and Jack do at his house sometimes. But Danny says there are things going on that I know nothing about, and I could tell from his expression he wasn't about to tell me.

It's all that Cindy's fault really. She's this girl Alan went out with for about a year, then she chucked him 'cos it wasn't gettin' anywhere. After that he started going away places all the time, and hardly ever sending us postcards. I never fancied Cindy much myself. She's 'got shape' and white hair that sticks up all over the place. I mean, I wouldn't exactly accuse her of being fat but you know what I mean. Definitely a borderline. Healthy people are always dead stupid-looking, I think. They always have sun-tans and bleached hair. They'll all be bald and wrinkled before they're thirty. At least, that's what Jack says, and I believe him.

The worst thing that happened was when my mum found those needles in his room. She said she wasn't snooping or anything. But I have my suspicions. I mean, she's never out of my room. I'm sure it might have been my fault, in a way. When Dad got back from the scout trip he said: 'That was a real shot in the arm.' My face must've changed or something 'cos they all looked at me, him and Mum and Danny and Alan, and I was about to say something, but didn't. But Mum found out anyway just after that. She found a bunch of needles in his bottom drawer and said, 'This is the last straw.' I agree that it's pretty horrible, sticking needles into yourself and your friend, but it's not as if he does it in front of her, or even when she's in the house – so there's no chance of her walking in on them unexpectedly.

I went into his room while he was packing his rucksack and just sat on the bed. I like Alan, and didn't want him to think that maybe I'd told her when he wasn't there. Though he doesn't actually know that I saw them that day. He hugged me and said he'd bring me something back from France or Amsterdam or Paris, wherever he was going. But I said it was OK, just to send a card. I had this awful feeling that he wouldn't be back and didn't want to build myself up for a present I would never get. Mum seemed relieved that he was going and I thought that was a bit mean of her. I mean, it's not Alan's fault that she isn't his mum. He doesn't have his own mum. I couldn't help thinking – though I know I'm not allowed to – that it would've been so much better if it was Danny who had been caught with needles in his bedroom.

When I grow up I'm not going to live in the same house as Danny. I might live with Jack and his mum, or just by myself. I'll still be a thin white girl, even when I'm all grown up and rich. I'll never change. You don't have to, you know. People just think that, 'cos they copy everyone else who does. They've just got no imagination, Jack says. And I believe him. I don't care what anyone says, I'll be a thin white girl for ever. I'll never marry anyone. I won't even love anyone. I'll never need anything, like drugs or cream cakes or shots in the arm. The only thing I'll ever want is money – and it's OK to want that. 'Money's your best friend, it doesn't betray you.' That's what they said in a film, the night they told us about Alan. Or it might've been 'your only friend'. It could've been that.

He sent me a card, but nobody else got one. He liked me. I'm a thin white girl. I never cried at the funeral. Thin white girls don't cry.

Me and Jack hardly go near the graveyard now. We don't play there at all. I guess we were bound to outgrow it. We got sick of the swing park ages ago.

I went on my own once to see Alan. His is just a small stone, but I like it. I'm glad he's been buried. I stood looking at the stone, and the words carved into it, and remembered something Jack said to me a long time ago.

'Never stand on somebody's left side,' he said, his face pinched and white. 'It's easier for them to stab you that way.'

I think he read it in a book. I don't know why I thought of that then. I stood for a long time staring at the new stone, trying to get the nerve to touch it. I must before leaving. He would know if I didn't bother to do it. I stood on until it was quite dark and my tea would be ready.

'Unless they're left-handed,' I said aloud. And I cried.

I cried all the way home, even though it looked dead stupid. I cried on and on and my mother ran out to the gate to meet me.

'What happened to you?' she asked. 'What's happened?'

'I fell,' I said, and kept on crying.

She took me inside and sat me on her knee and started asking the usual questions about Bad Men. I just nodded No and went right on crying. We sat for a while and finally I stopped.

'I'm frightened.'

'What of? There's nothing to be frightened of here I'm . . .'

'I'm frightened I'll not be a thin white girl any more.'

'Come on', she laughed, 'your dinner's ready.'

But I never told her where I'd been. And I never went back there. At least, not unless Jack was with me.

The Hotel Summer

The first room we stayed in was on the ground floor at the back. There were bars but only on one of the windows, which we left open to begin with. The smell eventually made us close it. The room was large and dusty and stuffy. I was frightened to let the sheets touch me but every night succumbed to a blissful dead sleep.

The toast was served by a half-caste in the basement. The dining room smelled as if someone had done the toilet in it five years ago, and not flushed, and left the window locked. The maid's skin made her look as if she didn't wash and the plate often had food stuck at the edges and was still damp from the hasty wash between us and the last person who'd eaten off it. But breakfast is the only supplied meal.

After three days on the ground floor at the back, they moved us while we were out to upstairs at the front. The toilet in this room flushed, but left things floating on top afterwards. Sometimes it was the paper I'd just put down, sometimes things I'd never seen before. The reason why they moved us was someone else was coming who always stays in room three. The manager told me this either just before or just after he invited me out to dinner.

First he said: 'Is that guy your boyfriend?'
'What guy?'
'The one you share the room with.'
'No,' I said.
Then he asked me to dinner.
'No, I never eat dinner.'

That's true enough. We can't afford it. We have a large bag of crisps and a bottle of Highland Spring because tap water gives you kidney trouble. But we wouldn't eat much in the summer anyway. It's too dirty.

The upstairs room was better, because it's best being up high, but it was only a comparative improvement. We couldn't wait to get out of there. The manager had our passports. We sat at night planning mad escapes. Jack could come in wearing a headover with eyes cut out and do a raid on the front desk and retrieve our kit. But if he was going to that trouble he'd be as well doing the till also. And there can't be much in it. Most people are waiting for social security cheques like us. When the giro comes we pay the bill and move somewhere better. That's the plan but when we pay the bill there will not be much left. And for a flat we need a deposit. And a month in advance. One of us has to get a job. Working is bad enough but working in the summer requires a regular shower and ice-cream when you want it and some clothes.

I get a job as a secretary and use the lunch hour calling everyone I know to help stop thinking about food. These people I know are from two years ago when I used to come to London for fun. They expect me in a plastic ballgown with dyed backcombed hair and big glass ear-rings. But now I wear cotton, military things that stay versatile. I have short hair so that I can wear it wet all the time without having to wash it. Though we keep having to buy razors. I wouldn't go round with a moustache anyway no matter how poor I was so we may as well shave our heads too. Buy a few extra razors for that. The worst thing is having to eat. And the water bill. If it wasn't for that we'd save faster.

That lunchtime chatter got me a result. I managed a freeload. Jack couldn't believe our luck. 'The cheque came today as well,' he said, when I met him after work and told him we could go and stay at Hartley's. Hartley lives in a pre-war council estate in East London. 'It has more charm than a Barratt home,' Jack said. It was the only nice thing he could think of. But Hartley took offence. He was disappointed with my hair and clothes. A few days later he said to me, 'Look, you can stay here but there isn't really much space. I mean, you can stay but there isn't room for him.'

Jack went to live in Holland Park for a while but people kept calling the police so he switched to Hyde. There's a lot of fruits in parks after dark but he keeps to himself. Once he had a conversation with a man who'd lost his dog but generally he just dives under a bush and bivets up.

'You look 124 years old,' I said to him after he'd been living there for a month.

'It's the tension,' he said.

Living in the park meant Jack couldn't get a giro – unless he wanted to queue all day. But if he queued all day he couldn't go shop-lifting. Which meant I had to buy him food, and myself, and razors, and a present to keep Hartley happy. And my wages are low. Less than £100 a week for a seven-hour day with a cabbage. The boss. The asswipe. The one I inevitably despise but don't want to corrupt myself thinking about it. I need three months' salary to afford a month in advance and a deposit and some cash for us until our housing benefit arrives once we move in and claim unemployment. Three months' salary isn't enough but it's all I can imagine in advance.

When the three months is up we can't find a place. We could get a room but there's no bathroom. It's worse than an almost-sleazy hotel. There's no breakfast, no phone. Jack prefers the park to this place we could get, if we wanted it, this room. And I prefer Hartley's. But I don't like Hartley's. I don't like Hartley. But I prefer Hartley's. I don't like being unemployed. I'm too poor. But it beats the cabbage. Solitude is best, even when it's poor solitude. Rich solitude would be better but I'm not stupid enough to think it's perfect. But I imagine it. I want it. It's my aspiration. What to do? 'Get motivated,' Jack says. How? 'Run, get yourself some sand.' He always carries thirty pounds of sand in his bergen. The SAS use bricks, but people get upset if you take their bricks. It's easier getting sand. Jack got his at a golf course late one night. He left me holding the extra spade while he piled it into his rucksack.

'What if it has beasts in it?' I ask. 'The more the better,' he says. He doesn't say.

I hate people who have no money. I hate people who have just a little money and they cling at it. They go in and out of their box and make a farce of their responsibilities. They have children and encourage it to go on. They poison themselves. They are lazy. They can't even be bothered to stand up straight. They're too tired.

We don't have to stay here?

Where do we go? We can't go back there. They hate us back there. They suspect us of being successful. Someone else's success is taken as a personal insult in Glasgow. Here they cover it up better. Sly enough to be ashamed of it. Besides, they want it for themselves. They want to linger round it. But we're not successful, they just imagine it in Glasgow.

We don't even know how to become successful. We just have white, innocent faces with clever eyes and brave mouths. We have unusually long fingernails and clean-cut habits. We're just a couple of kids.

We still have fun. We kick tramps, and run out of McDonald's without paying, and enter cinemas by the fire exit. The sort of things you do in summers. We have the same haircut and look like the same dream. The one everyone has. It only works sometimes. You're only young once. It can't last. They say that all the time in Glasgow, hoping.

Another hotel. But not a sleazy one, never another sleazy one. We've made up our mind. We'll find the money someplace. £70 per night. That's the standard. It isn't tasteful but it's clean. And has a video. Showing the same film all day. Then a new one the next day. Or a choice that day if you want to buy one. And free bubblebath, but breakfast's extra. Clean towels. Less frightening sheets. An arduous cleaner. White working-class waitress.

People are impressed when they meet me in the foyer. There's a chandelier and a high-tech lift. And a lot of Americans about. There's me in my military greens and combat cap over my hair and a red mouth on. A ruby ear-ring if I wear the thriller dress but the ear-rings are flat now. The thriller dress is when we're hopeful. The man I'm meeting is going to give me a contract. When you have a beautiful face it's your obligation to market it. I have no strong faith in my face but Jack does. He believes in it wholeheartedly. It's easier when it isn't your own.

There must be something you want to do.

They were always saying that. 'Something realistic,' my mother added.

'I do,' I said, 'I want to do lots.' But I couldn't give an example. 'Always give examples,' they write at the bottom of your composition. I can give a million examples of things I hate. But I don't want to be another negative. I hate that. Those weaklings, I think, sitting in my room. I can hear their television going. They're always at it. They know all the programmes. There's no fooling them when it comes to who's up to what.

First I went to a lot of parties. As many a night as possible. I met Jack at one of them. All his friends liked me. He didn't speak to me for two years. Then one day I saw him in a churchyard. I had followed him there, but he remains convinced it was coincidence. He was taking photographs of a pink marble tomb.

'They must have really loved each other,' he said. He meant the two names on the tomb. I hadn't known he was a romantic before. It made me feel less ashamed. But later it annoyed me. Two old romantics against the world. And then I knew. I have to get a practical man. Someone who's already got money or knows exactly how to get it. A dreamer's no use, even a motivated one. Even someone strong. Being sensitive and overcoming your fears is fine and honourable, but not having the fear at all: that's convenient. That's useful. That's a damned way towards success.

He guessed all this, he knew, but we stayed together during the hotel summer and a bit longer. Because he arranged an income, and we found a better hotel, and had wild arguments watching television. Because we wanted something else. Always waiting to get away from the present place into the next place, never getting rid of the last one. Blocking out the sounds of the outside, the people downstairs, each other. Worse, the awareness that they're there. The awful knowledge. I don't want any of it, I don't think dying's horrible. I think that's the biggest con. But I don't want to do it yet. Not until I try. I must know I was brave first, I did it, whatever it is. Still looking in the mirror checking my looks. Losing your looks, that mysterious happening described by my mother, her sisters, losing your looks happens when you least or most expect it.

We got up early in the less sleazy hotels. We got up around nine. We had to. We didn't know if we could afford another night. Or if they could keep us in the same room. Or if they'd have to move us to another room. The same décor, but a different number, which makes it confusing for me at night asking for the key, if I get back first, myself, without Jack. Jack always remembers the room number, I don't.

Jack is working now. 'It's my turn,' he said. He didn't tell me what. It's the best way. Some mornings he could pay the bill easily and we could stay another night, another two nights. Other days we had to go somewhere else and write a new cheque, because each place will only take one large cheque; and each new place will only take a £50 and a £20, two cheques. But there are plenty of places. Plenty of rooms at £70. Sometimes £65. The book has six cheques left in it. After that we get the rented room.

During the day if he's left money I buy something to eat. I buy a paperback. I take two baths usually, sometimes three. Taking a bath stops you feeling hungry. The water takes all the hunger away. So even if you had money you wouldn't eat anyway. Of course, it only works in the summer.

It was a hot summer. I had cotton clothes. I could wash them in the bath then borrow the hotel's iron. I got known around those hotels as the girl who was always after the iron.

A job for me? Complicated. Not impossible. I was a bit low on energy. But there were plenty of ads. I stole a newspaper once. I don't like stealing. It makes me nervous now. I usually get caught. The only things I don't mind stealing are the ones I don't need.

Leaving a forwarding is complicated. I have to give an old address and hope it will catch me up in time for the interview. Once it did! But I didn't have any cleans that day, and I was unhappy, and didn't want the job anyway. I'm lazy. And I hate communicating with people on a compulsory and inferior basis. I'm no good at work, at the phenomenon. In an actual placement they love me. I automate myself. Enact the perfect employee's part. That's all I can do. Otherwise it gets confused. They sit me down and say, 'We have no space for individuality.' Always it ends by me not turning up any more. They try to persuade me back sometimes. I can't. Then eventually I get another one. I have to. But it doesn't last either.

But the hotel summer was perfect for not working. I had food at least once a day, with Jack. I had my bath, a bed, and a change of scene every couple of days. Space in between time for the old romantic in me to flourish. To sit and think. To avoid the sun. To stay cool. To apply and touch up and wipe off and reapply that lipstick. I could do all those things. Uninterrupted. And at night Jack would turn up. He would turn up at odd moments of the day too. Or call. I'd get back and they'd hand me a Telephone Message paper in red and white. With blue ink, or black, which suits it better. I used to go out, walk to the park gate and back, then see if anyone had called in my absence.

These hotels are in Lancaster Gate. We moved along them one by one. Until we found the room. It amazed me how they could all look the same from outside and inside some were sleazy and dirty and others clean and middle-aged. Some give a breakfast, some don't. I started to get suspicious if it was only £50. Then we found one for £40. We didn't find it. We arrived at it, like the others. It was colonial. And clean. There was breakfast. Dinner at extra rate, but twice they forgot to bill us; we felt lucky there. But they couldn't keep us. They were fully booked for the summer. We got in on a cancellation. They'd keep us in mind for another. But we couldn't leave a forwarding.

The next place did a buffet breakfast. Cold cuts, croissants, toast you make yourself in a toaster. Big carafes of orange juice. Heaven. Yoghurt and fruit to take away. All in all, lots of gosh. They even had chocolate spread.

One night the manager, a man who wore a mustard nylon neck under his desk suit, speaks to Jack on his way in. 'We must ask you to leave. It's your wife,' he says, 'she steals food from the dining room. She lies in her room all day eating it.'

'How do you know what she does?'

'I know. There are crumbs.' (It was a Swedish hotel.) 'And the empty wrappers in her bin – chocolate spread, our yoghurts. It is forbidden to carry food to your room.'

Jack stared at him.

'The maid has seen it – and the housekeeper!'

'OK,' Jack said. 'We'll leave.'

Where do we go next? What do we have in mind? How long do we want to stay? We don't know.

(What age are we? What are our plans for the next five years? Who are our referees?)

What do you want from life? Who told you to say that? (Think.) Persistent clichés making me uneasy amidst the demented trivia.

We go to live in the room. Jack doesn't stay long. The worst thing when the hotel summer was over. I knew it could never happen again. I could think it was happening, but it wouldn't be. But why would I want it to?

What are you going to do when you're thirty?

They're always asking me what I'm going to do when I'm thirty. When I was sixteen I said, 'Die,' utterly convinced. When it gets nearer you think, How am I going to die? Then you know you're not, you haven't got the guts, you're a coward like the rest, and anyway you want to See What Happens. That's what Jack says. 'I don't want to die, I want to wait and see what happens.' He means historically, I think. The other thing they say is, *What do you do all day?* Believe me, the time passes. Passing time is not a problem. It's the easiest part. The goddamned mystery.

'I read books,' I say, but it's a lie. I get books. From the library, off people. I buy paperbacks. Ones I've heard of, ones I like the look of. But I don't read them. I pile them impressively about the room. And note in my diary when the library ones are due back. Then I take them back. I walk through the park to the library, or take the underground when it's raining. God knows why, I like rain. Avoiding it's just a habit. Usually there are one or two little duties like that per day. At least one. Sometimes the whole damn day is full of them. Picking up the laundry, buying water, looking at the job ads. That takes longest. I have to get the paper first, then circle all the 'likelys' in red, then read through them more carefully, then prepare a c.v. when I'm in the mood. And queue at the post office if I'm going to send it. All that takes about two and a half days. Sometimes longer. Sometimes I cut the ads out, but don't read them for a week or so, then I think: it's too late now, someone else will have the job by now anyway.

Do you have a television? That's another one. No, I don't. Well, what do you do? I don't know what to say. Sleep? But I don't sleep much. Not like I used to. I'm in bed a lot, but I'm not sleeping. I'm lying there. I think about getting up. I used to get up and raid the kitchen. But I don't have a kitchen with this room. I don't have to cook. I don't have a bathroom, either, but I need to wash. I need to go downstairs and stand in the shower in my shoes, trying not to breathe in or touch the edges. I read everything there is about AIDS. Go through all the newspapers and current affairs mags in Smith's. They hate you fingering the papers, because they get all crushed and untidy. But nobody says anything. The magazines you can read all day, if you like, but I get fed up standing. And none of the articles interest me much anyway. Except the stuff about AIDS. And that's repetitive. There was one bit that scared me. Because I'd already worried about it in secret. So reading it made me shitless. It was when Norman Fowler said the virus could get stronger. Then celibacy is no protection. You get it from breathing and eating ice-cream and all those normal everyday activities like getting an Irvine Rusk haircut and going to the movies. That's what I do. I spend a great deal of time in the cinema. I go in and sit and think all through the film. Unless it's Matthew Modine. I love alliterated names, and clean-cut types. When it's a clean-cut type, I don't think, I imagine it's myself. (In the movie, in their life.) *Do you have a boyfriend?* That's another one. The term embarrasses me. I mean, what if he's not a boy. But saying manfriend would be just as bad. Like ladyfriend. No, I don't have a boyfriend. But sometimes pretend to. That satisfies them. Now they know I spend all my spare time fucking this boyfriend. This enigma they haven't met yet, or aren't likely to. I'm keeping him all to myself. I'm living for him. I love him to death. All I want to do is fuck this boyfriend.

People used to ask sometimes, 'Are you gay?' But it's getting rude to ask that again. For a while it was fashionable. Tame decadence. Now it's a plague. The ill-luck of the fag. A fruit's worse than a flesh-eater. Covering it up makes it worse.

Well, she is a looker, they say, behind my back, when I'm not listening. That's compensation, I suppose. She can live with her face a little while. The thin hard body. But it's impossible to know that you are beautiful. The closest you get is to suspect. Have it insisted by others. And it can only fade. Research shows that only average women cling on to their looks. Beauties know right away it's a waste of time. Some of them try to get it over with quickly. Others ignore it. Burn-out or apathy.

There are some things I like. Men with good arms. The hills at night-time, with the air and cold stars and everyone else dead. Chocolate is a repetitive pleasure. And red lipstick. And whiteness. And going to the movies alone. Clean-cut types a reliable trivia. Scientists with sun-glasses a diversion. In bed all afternoon alone. Not listening to anything. Perhaps using a silver spear to clean behind my fingernails. Undisturbed. And knowing no one is going to come. For the slightest reason. New Year's

Day is great for that. Even the most lonely of your acquaintances are too proud to offer themselves then. They assume you are busy with the family, boyfriend and box of shortbread. They feel ashamed.

Accept your solitude, enjoy, I want to say, but they think me weird enough as it is. They say I'm strange. If it wasn't for the looks and imaginary boyfriend I'd be shunned. How are you supposed to know when you're strange? Unless somebody tells you. And how do you know they're right? People keep telling me. You're unnatural. You're mad. How do they know? What do they mean? What do they think I'll do?

After the hotel summer I went to the room with Jack. The room with the kitchen and bath. Then Jack went and I went to the room. Where I hadn't much to do. Those government cheques paid for it. I lay in bed listening to the relentless scuttle, thinking I must get away from here. I wanted to get away. Later on I married a comparatively dull man and we talked about having two children. This man is not dull in everyone's eyes; he is duller than Jack. (Who is interesting.) Jack went to Belize on a six-month military mission. He disappeared after four months and was not seen by me again.

Practically Park Lane

I almost live in Mayfair. One night I went to a laundry. I met this woman. She said something to me. She said, 'You know you've got a really great face.' Normally I wouldn't answer. At night in a laundry I would stare ahead like I heard nothing. But this was a woman.

'Thank you,' I replied. My washing was in the drier otherwise I would take a walk next. I can take a walk while it's in the washer. That's a twenty-five min. cycle. But I like to keep opening the drier door, to remove what's dry. It goes quicker that way. So my grandfather's wife tells me when I call long distance.

'You know you really ought to do something with that face of yours.' By this time I was glancing at the windows, trying to catch my reflection outside.

'Thanks,' I said again. I knew she was looking at me. I couldn't see her wash anywhere. There was a washer going, but it was a man's wash. I saw him put it in. She could be collecting it for him?

'You know you'll be more comfortable if you sit.'

'Oh, I like standing.'

'Why's that?'

'No reason.'

'You just like it. I understand that.'

I walked over to the door. My wash can't be long. I thought about taking it home before it was dry, but decided that would be silly. There's nowhere to hang it.

She joined me at the door. She was low and thick and a bit foreign.

'That's quite a voice you have.'

'Thanks.'

'But it's the face. That's a great face.'

'If I'd had a face like that . . . who knows?'

Saying thank you again would be inappropriate.

'You know! That's just the sort of face I could take home with me.'

'Well I hope you don't do that,' I said, staring along the street. No one seemed to be watching us. There were some types on the pavement opposite, drinking beers and vino blanco. I made up my mind there and then to use the laundry service next time.

'Not tonight,' she said, 'but maybe someday, huh? Not this time but maybe next time. See ya!'

When I woke up next morning it was damp and cold but I needed the electricity for my hair. Washing my hair in the shower frightens me. Not many of the tenants use the shower, but I need to be clean. There's a sink in my room in full view of the windows across the street, so people can see if they're looking. They're foreign. I asked my landlord for a curtain that fits and he said 'OK', but hasn't provided one so far. His name's Hosie. He drives a white sports car and goes to the Limelight wth Oli Mullens, his partner. He's a rotten dancer but I like white cars. Cars are like gloves and men and underwear. They have to be white or black.

I haven't been inside a club in months. I can't afford it, but that's no excuse. Really it's because I don't want to go. I used to enjoy showing off and wear my hair white and dance very well on Mondays. My grandfather has this theory people always get what they want. I wanted to be popular then so I was. Now I'm like this. When I want something else, things will change.

Like a husband, for example. I met a man the other day who would do. I'm seeing him for dinner so who knows? I'll wear something classic and get my shoes heeled for the occasion. I don't know what we'll talk about. He might kiss me on the mouth. But only if an opportunity arises. 'You can't do much in this life without opportunity.' My grandfather's wife said that.

I met the man outside the post office. He had on a made-to-measure coat and was holding a designer umbrella like he was embarrassed. He isn't foreign, but has this dark look. I was grinning, he thought it was at him. It was raining pretty heavily by now. I didn't have a coat, but was smiling partly through nerves, partly because I had just got away with something.

Inside the post office there are four phone booths. One of them's Cardphone. One's out of order and the other's 999 only. So there's a queue for the normal one, but that morning I got right in and used it immediately. I was trying to fix a lunch with someone. Before I left the booth I saw this purse stuck on the ledge under the phone. It must be empty, I thought. But it made a noise when I picked it up.

Then I started worrying. What if the woman behind me owned the purse? It looked like an old woman's purse. She could be waiting there to search the booth when I'm done. Old people are like that. She could be watching me fingering it, and be waiting her chance. Too sneaky to confront me directly, she won't be above informing the clerk behind the grid on me.

And what if it's not her purse, it's someone's. I could take it home then find a photograph inside. Or worse, a bit of hair or an old tooth.

But then I thought take it, don't be a coward. So I took the cash out quickly and left the post office, grinning.

The man on the pavement is a dentist who hasn't been in London long. His practice is nearby. His opening line is, 'What wonderful incisors, I'd love to X-ray those sometime.' Normally I wouldn't share a strange man's umbrella, or drink coffee in a dental surgery. It's not every day I steal a purse either. So I go with this dentist and we arrange that date. He didn't X-ray my teeth though. Not this trip.

*

A Month On

It's ten minutes to twelve. He doesn't like it when I laugh loud. It makes him feel threatened. The reason I was laughing: a guy I used to know with strange ears has a photograph album and in it there's this snapshot – taken in a club – of a girl I know now, wearing a tail. I met her by chance at the Angel yesterday. I don't know why she's wearing a tail in that photograph. Except it was that sort of club. Everyone dressed to thrill then pretended to have spent *nothing* on their outfit. To have made it themselves with an old curtain or got it at Paddy's for ten pence. But no one else wore a tail, and I wanted to ask Elle why she had, but I didn't. We talked about London clubs and which of the Glasgow expatriates you're most likely to see in them. I meet more on the street now. I walk everywhere because of the Underground and the funny experience I had in a black cab once. The driver didn't give me change. I got out of the car and started to run because I was in Whitechapel. Jack the Ripper country to me at the time. The driver got out and ran as well. I went into Ivan's building and said, 'Oh no,' to the ethnic waiting for the lift then took the nineteen flights in a few seconds less than a minute. I used to do karate routines in that lift.

Inside Ivan's door, which has an upside-down lock, I had a debate with a fruit (also staying there) about whether or not to call the police about that mad cabbie. We stood right behind the door, which we'd snibbed, and he said, 'Someone may find herself in the same spot.' I said fuck, intelligently, then Ivan tried to unlock the door with his key but it was bolted. He called through the letter box, 'It's me,' but we had already run shrieking to the kitchen and locked all the windows in case that cabbie had a rope, or it's a poltergeist.

Eventually Ivan got in by releasing the bolt by putting his hand through the letter box. He made us stale wholemeal toast and the fruit didn't take butter with his.

Ivan is no longer in Whitechapel. He's in Brixton. I am in the horrid bit of Mayfair but everyone says 'Mmhm W1' when I give my address and wonder who I'm fucking because I don't have my own money. I never fucked Ivan but the girl with the tail did once. He went strongly bi soon after (though there's no connection) until 1985, when he was 70:30 in favour of girls. By 1986 he was straight again. I don't blame him. He calls me 'the most camp girl' but I'm a natural ascetic and AIDS and herpes and contraceptual cancers are just excellent excuses for me. I have unfulfilled physical fantasies and use my energy being intellectually decadent.

Occasionally I decide to solve the cash flow problem once and for all. And recently started this scheme with the celibate dentist.

We walk along the street eating an ice-cream sundae. The sort from Baskin Robbins. I have strawberry, he has chocolate, both with fudge sauce, nuts, cherries, whipped cream and a pink spoon. He's really into his and doesn't believe my plan anyway. People passing either smile chattily or look superior. On a darker cross-street I slug my sundae into the face of an oncoming city type, grab his case, and go. The dentist waits apologetically beside the man sprawled on the pavement for a few seconds then comes after me.

There isn't much in the case. But we do it again and get some cash. The dentist is into it. Wants to do it all the time. He lets me keep the cash but wants to be the one to throw. I let him throw. He leaves the cherries on top of his sundae. 'Don't you think it achieves a better effect that way?' he asks. I tell him we have to at least change the B&R. But he must do it the same way every time or he's lost his thrill. What an asswipe. I know I must get rid of him and start looking for a new place to live. I don't find one because really I'm used to central heating and a full deep freeze and even the horrible bit of Mayfair's better than Brixton for someone like me.

The dentist gets thrills elsewhere also. He changes every filling in my mouth to Occlusin. He does it on Sunday morning, when the surgery is empty, telling me each time, 'This treatment would cost . . .' showing brochures from America, the spotlight that makes a patient relax, and what pure cocaine can do to enamel.

And the fish. I once was on a bus and overheard a woman describe her husband's infatuation with his pet fish.

'But how bad is it?' the woman with her asks.

'Bad enough, he never touches me.'

'But does he do it with it? Does he impregnate his fish?'

'There's more than one,' the distressed woman says, 'there's bloody millions of them.'

I wonder. I have heard of a practice of swallowing live fish whole and ejaculating simultaneously but of course haven't tried it. I can't remember the official name now.

'Do you like your fish?' I ask the dentist.

'Of course they're an excellent relaxation aid – innovative colours too, don't you think?' All innovations must be corroborated by me.

Of course I can't be seen with him. He'd tell everyone about the ice-cream dodge. And what if he met the tail. He'd be laughing loudly then. He'd be getting one for himself. He'd come in and say, 'Will you sew this on to my bum, I'll freeze it first.' Then he'd go on and on until I got out a needle and thread and Hey-ho. Fuck. What a wacko. What an asshole. Why do idiots end up with incomes and comfortable flats?

Eventually I have always found if you don't lift a finger to seek an escape from your unbearable situation one presents itself anyway.

MATTHEW FRANCIS

Green Winter

It is dark when the guards come to wake me. For a moment, I imagine that I am back home, and that some catastrophe has taken place, a fire, perhaps, or a burglary, but then I remember and swear at them. Yuri grins and says, 'Come with us. The Chairman has visitors.'

Outside, the stars have already faded, and the only light comes from a few scraps of muddy snow. The white winter is over and the green winter is beginning; it has been thawing for a week now, and I tread carefully to avoid the deep, slushy puddles which are scattered everywhere, colder than snow itself. I must be still half-asleep, because a line of English poetry suddenly appears in my head:

> Woken in the pre-dawn by my guards . . .

Where does it come from? Have I read it somewhere?

The Chairman smiles, just like Yuri, and says, 'Come in, come in, please take a seat. A cold morning for the time of year, isn't it?'

'It isn't morning,' I tell him sullenly.

It is warm in the office. There is a charcoal stove, a big one, and an electric light, though without a shade. To make it look more like an office and less like a caretaker's hut, there is a desk with a typewriter on it, and one of those wire in-trays you see in Moscow offices. I am not deceived, however. Tigran Vartanovitch is not in favour. Zhelatsk is not one of those modern camps they have further west, with space for 5,000 prisoners, closed-circuit television, and central heating in the guards' quarters. It is the true end of the world, *ultima Thule*. The Chairman must have said the wrong thing at a cocktail party, or perhaps he was at the wrong cocktail party altogether.

I am given a cup of coffee, which scalds my palate and tastes, enigmatically, of paraffin, but for which I am grateful. The Chairman introduces me to his visitors, a tall, athletic, bald man from Budapest (Dr Koshka) and a small, crumpled, bald man from Moscow (Dr Simagin). Koshka, the Hungarian, is an eminent parapsychologist, and Simagin a representative of the Supreme Committee for the Advancement of Soviet Science – in other words, I assume, some sort of policeman, even if an inductive rather than a deductive one. They ask me a number of questions about what they refer to as my 'powers'.

'I have no powers,' I tell them impatiently.

I have no powers. When it comes to clairvoyance, I am just as likely to be spectacularly wrong as spectacularly right. If I had powers, after all, I would be making a fortune in black-market beef carcasses or selling secrets to the Americans instead of languishing in this desolate place, this Thule, the period of cosmography, the blank zone on the map. Unfortunately, I cannot control the visions that come to me when I lie in my hut at night, any more than I can control the cold or the darkness. Knowledge is only power if it is knowledge that somebody wants, and mine is not. Sometimes I wonder if even I want it.

Recently, my visions have been of a man of about forty, handsome in a craggy way, an Englishman, a poet. Sometimes I see him in bed with a blonde, frail woman, the wife of his publisher. (He addresses her as Ro, a curious syllable which might be the Greek letter or the English word for fish eggs.) They argue frequently about literary awards, about travel grants he might get to go to Iceland or America, about a man called Simpkins of whom the poet is jealous. At other times, I see him in village halls, or in cold, varnish-scented seminar rooms, reading impassioned descriptions of his childhood to sparse audiences of uncomfortable and adoring females. Sometimes again, he is doing something mundane, like going to the lavatory or buying razor blades, but I see him with such vividness that I *am* the poet, I smell the soap or see the sunlight fall across the foreign money in the till. I am not myself. It is my only distinction that I am not always myself.

It is typical of my unevenness that, although the visitors are obviously interested in my spiritual, not my family life, my famous intuition at once leads me to believe that something has happened to Yelyena. Either she has received permission to go into exile – I mean the real kind, external exile – or she has been arrested, or she is dead. Dead – I am sure it is the latter. I do not know whether a political death or whether she has just died of something, but the voice has spoken.

On the contrary, Simagin tells me I am to be asked to take part in an experiment in the interests of the health and happiness of the Soviet people. For me, it will mean a transfer to Moscow, visits from Yelyena and the children, an end to the hard labour which is ruining my health. Dr Koshka, who is the Professor of Parapsychology at Moscow State Technical College, has assembled more than a hundred gifted psychics for the experiment, which involves, Simagin implies, our national security. Of course, what I learn in this hut is to go no further.

Simagin now becomes rhetorical and refers to great leaps that are being made in the name of Soviet science by beings whom he does not further define. Then Koshka takes over, and asks for the light to be extinguished so that he can show a film. The Chairman, excitingly, dismisses the guards, and a white, flickering square, a Thule, is projected on to the wall as Koshka struggles with the film. Now he has it. A luminous countdown flashes past: *10-9-8-7-6-5-4-3-2-1*. The film begins.

Scene One. Koshka, three or four years younger, walks down a Moscow street with a large red question mark poised over his head.

VOICE OVER: Have you ever wished you could do something with the unused parts of the brain?

Close-up of puzzled frown behind Koshka's horn-rimmed spectacles. Cut to:

Scene Two. Very dingy studio set intended to represent a laboratory. Two Soviet scientists, identified as such by white coats and Order of Lenin round neck, are pouring frothing liquid into test-tubes.

VOICE OVER: Soviet scientists have been labouring night and day to liberate the full power of the brain for the sake of science, socialism, and the advancement of humanity.

Cut to:
Scene Three. Old black-and-white film of Egyptian desert, clearly from pirated travelogue.

VOICE OVER: This is a pyramid.

'What was that about pyramids?' I ask, as someone behind me scrabbles to find the light switch. The bulb explodes metaphorically above my head, and the Chairman, ignoring my question, says, 'I hope you found that interesting.'

'But it's only just started.'

'What do you mean?' the Chairman demands, but Koshka squats in front of my chair and peers curiously into my eyes.

'What was the last scene you remember?' he asks. The question is so simple that I have a horrible feeling there must be a catch in it, but I reply anyway.

'The pyramids.'

'You've been asleep!' the Chairman says indignantly.

'Is that so?' Koshka asks. 'Have you been asleep?'

'No. Yes. No, not asleep.'

'Not asleep? Absent, perhaps?'

'Yes,' I reply, 'absent.'

*

After all, it is not easy to live in a mosaic. If Koshka had not squatted in front of my chair and searched my eyes as he did, I would not know myself why I missed the film. It is like clambering out of a dream and then, when you finally emerge, being unable to remember whether you had the dream last night or the night before, or whether it was a dream at all. There are only the little coloured stones to be fitted in somewhere.

For most of the film, I now realize, I was in England with the poet, who was in bed with a woman – his own wife, this time, rather than someone else's. Her name is Tess, and she differs from his other monosyllabic lover in almost every respect. Where Ro is blonde, Tess is dark. Where Ro has bony shoulders, Tess, from what I have been able to see of her above the duvet, is rather buxom. But her post-coital temper is just as fierce as Ro's. (It is a disappointment to me that I always seem to arrive in my other existence just after the fun has stopped and end up doing the agonizing instead of the ecstasizing.) Tess was reproaching me for my infidelity, which she claimed was very immature. I defended myself on the grounds that Ro is better placed than almost anybody in England to advance my career. In bed, she is a *femme de lettres* in her own right. She has had sex with all sixteen members, male and female, of the Firm, the group of poets who run the literary scene from their country houses in Oxfordshire and Gloucestershire, and thus has the power to cause domestic disharmony on a Parnassian scale. Poets are nothing if not domestic animals.

My English self, of course, is no exception to this rule, but he is not afraid that Tess will leave him. She is proud of his status as the leading poet of his generation and the likely next member of the Firm. The blood of Shakespeare and Milton flows in his veins, as she sees it, and, indeed, she is probably right. In any case, the poet talked so convincingly about his power over Ro and Ro's power over the English literary world that she finally fell asleep with a glow of enthusiasm suffusing her as far down as the sternum. The poet, however – or was it me by this time? – was not so sure. But then poets never are.

The photograph which Koshka hands me is of a grey-haired man, smiling in an eminent way as if discreetly attempting to show off his gold fillings.

'Do you know this man?' Koshka asks. I shake my head.

'You are sure?'

'Yes.'

'You would not like to guess his name? His nationality? Anything about him?'

'No.'

Koshka seems disappointed. He runs his hand over his scalp and begins to pace up and down.

'I am sorry you missed my film', he says eventually. 'I would show it again, but it will be dawn soon, and the curtains here would probably not be adequate to keep out the light. Never mind. Let me tell you something about myself.'

He continues walking very rapidly, more like a man on a military training exercise than one struggling with a train of thought. He explains that the film showed how he, Koshka, had had a mysterious vision of the shooting of a certain president in a foreign country, how he reported it to his local party and was ridiculed, and how the president was, in fact, assassinated several months later. How Koshka always remembered afterwards exactly where he was when he heard the news (in Dnyepopetrovsk railway station, returning from an International Conference on the Psychopathology of Dissidence). How he took the next train to Moscow instead of going home, and went straight to the offices of the Supreme Committee, where he explained what had happened, and how he was, after the necessary checks had been made, offered the Chair of Parapsychology, the first of its kind in the history of Soviet further education. How he conducted experiments in levitation, teleportation, telepathy and clairvoyance. Finally, the film showed his major finding, that a large number of gifted individuals concentrating their psychic forces on a single target could produce extraordinary effects, both physical and psychological.

Koshka stops his pacing and directs my attention to the photograph again.

'Suppose such a man were the target,' he says.

'Who is he?'

'Suppose he were the ambassador of a foreign power hostile to the Soviet Union.'

'Yes?'

'Suppose, then, that more than a hundred of the most gifted psychics in the country were gathered together in one place – Moscow State Technical College, for the sake of argument – and that they knew a great deal about the man. They might have done some research, and found out that he had a mistress back home in Wisconsin (or wherever he came from) to whom he still wrote occasionally; that as a boy he was sickly and suffered from rheumatic fever; that he once dreamed of being a professional basketball player but was not tall enough; that his mother was dying of Parkinson's disease; that the food he missed most in his present posting was corned beef. You understand the kind of information I mean?'

'I think so.'

'The kind it takes to know a man thoroughly. Suppose these gifted individuals knew such a man in this way, and that they used their knowledge against him. Suppose they concentrated on him for an hour a day, trying to influence him, to change his behaviour. What do you think would happen?'

'I don't know.'

'Might he make a mistake? Perhaps send a letter to his president full of erroneous information?'

'I don't know.'

'Alternatively, might he walk into the nearest police station and ask for political asylum?'

'I don't know.'

'Finally, might he not fall unexpectedly ill? Have a stroke, or suffer from hallucinations?'

'I don't know. How do you expect me to know?'

'I don't expect it,' Koshka replies, smiling. 'We don't know, either.'

*

A study. I know it is a study although I have never been in one before. Through a small window opposite the door, I can see some typical English scenery of a green variety, downland or heath or moorland – I am not familiar with the technical vocabulary. There is a single bed, suitable for throwing oneself upon when worn out by the act of creation, and also a desk, brilliant and significant in the disc of light thrown by an anglepoise lamp (even though it is daylight beyond the window). The walls are heavy with books. A man of about forty, handsome in a craggy way, is sitting at the desk writing a poem:

> Woken in the pre-dawn by my guards . . .

It is to be a political poem, a protest against the injustice of the Soviet system. It will be thick with authentic detail, black bread, small green fish eaten whole, tattered cloths bound round the feet instead of shoes. It will be tense with a reticent British courage, and it will win a major poetry competition because of its realism and political awareness:

> . . . I ask nothing
> But time to dream of my childhood,
> The odour of crushed blackberries,
> Sausage and soap and forgotten love affairs.
> But there is not very much time. Dawn is breaking.

Dawn is breaking as I explain to Dr Koshka and Dr Simagin that I am obliged to refuse their offer. The reason I give is not political or even moral. I explain that I am an individualist and do not think I could work well with other psychics, that the substance inside me doesn't appear to mix. Also that, as I remarked earlier, my faculties are passive ones and I have never influenced anybody to do anything in my life. It may be so, of course. The thought crosses my mind that I have perhaps influenced an English poet whose name I still do not know to write a poem about me that would never otherwise have been written. An alternative and more uncomfortable thought is that I may, in fact, have no objective existence outside his poem, and that this may explain my refusal to act in my own best interests – a common failing of fictional characters.

Koshka seems neither angry nor disappointed. He has, after all, more than a hundred psychics for his experiment. The guards are summoned again to take me to breakfast. As we leave the hut, a small, remote sun is shining, and the icy green of the surrounding fields looks suddenly foreign.

Demonland

Oposso, the 'civilized' southern tip of Kuovala. I lay on my hotel bed, unable to sleep because of the clatter of the electric fan and a visit I had just had from two members of President Le Bouqin's secret police. I was reading a book by Julian, an esoteric computer textbook about demons and debugging techniques.

'When a demon is enabled, it fires. If enabled while another demon is in the process of firing, however, it must wait for the prior demon to finish. A demon may be temporarily disabled in order to allow another demon to fire, but only three demons may be held in core in a disabled state at any one time. If several demons having equal priorities are enabled at the same time, they are executed in an arbitrary order and then disabled . . .'

Clattering words. Somehow, the two policemen who called on me that night had got hold of Julian's book, and wanted to know about it, about him. They already knew that he had disappeared. Quite possibly, he was in one of their own dungeons, telling everything he knew about disablement and arbitrary executions. Or possibly not. Perhaps they wanted to find him as much as I did. At any rate, the fact that he was an intellectual who wrote books they couldn't understand marked him down as a potential subversive in their eyes. They were nervous, pompous little men who had grafted a layer of CIA American on to their clanging Kuovalan accents and kept calling me 'you guy'. They had apparently taken the stuff about demons personally – 'What is demon, hey? You know demons?'

A new sound competed with the fan now, a soft whooping like that of a swanee whistle. It was the girasol, or north wind, which had blown every night since my arrival in Kuovala a week before. The local people believe it carries the voices of spirits exiled for terrible crimes to the inhospitable north of the island, inhabited only by Communist guerrillas and brown Stone Age villagers. It was the same solemn whistling which woke me on my first night here; Murgh lay beside me, breathing hard as if running in her sleep from the imaginary spirits. A strand of black hair across her face flickered and trembled. 'Julian,' she murmured, 'Julian . . .' and rolled over.

Next morning she denied it. She was only what the Kuovalans call a jazz girl, very elegant and very ignorant, who made her living from the American oilmen and construction engineers of Smith and Van Allen. That first evening, she had floated on to the next bar stool, smiled and said, 'I Murgh,' with such assurance that I thought for a moment it was a verb. A girl like that could easily have known Julian – probably she knew several – but it was strange, all the same, that she should murmur anyone's name in her sleep. Except her own: 'I Murgh . . .'

Julian was my employee, a nomadic programmer who wandered all over the world advising customers how to get the best out of their computer systems. At the time he disappeared, he was working for Strom's, an engineering firm who were trying to build a road between Smith and Oposso in the face of great and typically Kuovalan difficulties. Strom's, in common with most of our customers, had liked Julian; he was so nervous, shaggy and unpunctual that he would have looked like a brilliant programmer even if he hadn't actually been one. Brilliant he certainly was, but not dangerous, surely? Why should Le Bouquin or anyone else want Julian to disappear?

'The best way to eradicate bugs is by a system of prophylaxis. When bugs become aware that they will not be tolerated, they seldom develop. The ideal bugless program would be one that contained no code at all. In view of the impossibility of this, programmers would do best to aim at a state of *virtual codelessness*.'

At some point while reading Julian's book, I must have fallen asleep, but it didn't seem to make any difference. The words kept on spinning through my head, relentless in their meaninglessness, like the clattering of the electric fan, like the voices of the spirits in the girasol.

The grim Norwegian project manager knew all about bugs, though he pronounced them 'bogs'.

'Is all focking bogs,' he told me, 'bogs and focking yongle.' We ate fish curry with coconut milk in a tin hut whose walls shook and rang with the heat, and the project manager talked with monotonous fatalism about the three years he had spent in the yongle. Oddly enough, there is no real jungle in Kuovala, only a rocky Pacific *maquis* full of thorns and tough roots, of bright poisonous flowers that look like insects and insects that look like flowers. The project manager had two hundred men scheduled to do two years' work in the next six months. Of these two hundred, seventeen had dysentery, six gonorrhoea, and two had run off to join the Communists. After lunch, he took me to have a look at the road; dizzy with heat, chilli and singing tin walls, I followed him along two miles of smouldering asphalt, first smooth, then cracked by vines and creepers. At the end of the road, we stood and watched a blue butterfly palpitate on a branch. Only twelve miles beyond the butterfly was Oposso. Shadows shivered and leaves buzzed between us and the Kuovalan equivalent of civilization.

'Did Julian seem worried to you?'

'He was always worried, you know. He was serious man, thinking always a lot. Very good at bogs.'

'He wrote a book about them.'

'*Demons and Debogging Techniques*. I have one in the hot. Is impossible to onderstand.'

The butterfly was the size of a sparrow, but absurdly fragile. It appeared preoccupied, as if eating something on the branch, but there was nothing it could be eating. The project manager told me about the 'yazz girl' who had hung round with Julian for several weeks before he disappeared.

'He was not a kind of man for women, you know, only for bogs, and she didn't speak English. He sat on a rock writing programs and she would be stroking his hair.'

There had been two pimps as well, little men who looked like Kuovalans but talked like Americans and asked a lot of questions. The project manager thought Julian hadn't taken much notice of them; he was too busy worrying about bugs.

Bugs, I thought, how could anyone not worry about bugs in an island like this? As if worrying about that shivering, buzzing twelves miles of yongle would turn it into Chiswick High Road. The butterfly was within a few inches of my face. When I reached out a finger, very gently, to touch it, it gave a tiny shudder and bit me.

Julian's demons fluttered round my bed. They had long tapering heads which made them look as if they were wearing night-caps, and they changed colour continually: red, flame-yellow, butterfly blue. One carried a machine gun which it fired at my head in brief, malicious bursts. (I learned to recognize it, and to flinch when it approached.) Occasionally, a demon was disabled. When this happened, it would flutter wearily to the floor, where it lay twitching until it was re-enabled. President Le Bouquin stood in the shadows, a bald, brown-skinned presence in khaki, smiling to himself.

'You wake,' said Murgh. She was sitting on the bed in the half-darkness.

'How long have I been here?'

She held up three fingers.

'Three what? Days? Weeks?' But she didn't answer.

'You bit butterfly,' she told me.

'Yes, I remember. Where am I?'

'This Smith. Doctor soon.'

When the doctor did call, there was something ominous about his expression that made me ask him suddenly if I was dying.

'Slowly, like the rest of us,' he replied with a forced chuckle.

He was one of those Edwardian Americans, a tall, bald man with a curling moustache and a deep, thoughtful voice. Whatever he was worried about, he hid it well.

That evening, I found Julian's book beside my bed. I had another try at it, but with no success. Like the little men who had called at the hotel that evening, and whom I equated (wrongly?) with the two pimps who had hung around the Strom's construction site while the yazz girl stroked Julian's hair, I kept taking his bugs and demons personally. They had made an appearance in my dreams, after all. As I read, I assigned to each of them a pinched little Kuovalan face; like a novelist, I tried to discover the motive behind their actions. They must have some reason for all this enabling and disabling, this firing and executing, I thought to myself, otherwise why do it? Of course, in my saner moments I was aware that this was absurd, and that there was no motive, only the logic of the program.

Next morning, the camp was in a panic which nobody tried to hide. Through the walls of the hut, I could feel people running about with random urgency so unceasing and desperate that it was exhausting to listen to. At lunchtime, the doctor told me that I was to be moved to Van Allen right away. Eventually, he admitted that there were rumours of a Communist raid on Smith. The government had been alerted, and had promised to send troops along the coast road via Van Allen, but no one knew when they would arrive.

'You'll be safer in Van Allen,' the doctor said. 'You're still suffering some residual toxaemia as a result of the butterfly, but there's no reason why you shouldn't travel. A sick man will only be a liability here, and it wouldn't be good for your condition to be shot at.'

'Nor for yours,' I told him, but he shrugged and replied that you couldn't dismantle a whole oilfield, even if you wanted to. So after lunch, they put me on a stretcher, and two Kuovalan labourers carried me along a sickening bumpy road that got further and further from Smith without getting nearer to anywhere else. Shadows shivered, leaves buzzed, but I could no longer tell whether they were inside my head or outside. From time to time, I would call out to the labourers, to ask them how much further, but they trudged on silently like mummies in a horror film, as the sweat stains darkened their T-shirts.

By the time I realized they were taking me to the Communists, I was too ill to care.

For many days I sat as if hypnotized on the floor of the cave in which I was being held prisoner. I was CIA vampire, worm on hide of popular state, chap who dared defy will of People Marxist Socialist Army Kuovalesque. At mealtimes I ate dried saltfish curry and drank Kuovalan bottled beer with its alarming petrol-and-blackberries taste. At night the fire threw big military shadows on the wall of the cave, and I imagined they were President Le Bouquin's men come to rescue me. But nobody came, except specially selected soldiers with recantations for me to sign. The recantations were difficult to understand, but I signed all of them. They bore the name G. L. Fredora, either as a letterheading or underneath the text, as the names of company directors appear on business stationery.

'Julian imperialist traitor, is?' my guard said eagerly when I asked him, 'we are all very well known.' Apparently Julian had lived in the camp for several weeks and had seemed willing to join them permanently, though he was still, even in the absence of a computer, preoccupied with his bugs. Suddenly, however, he had disappeared; the guard was still quite bitter about it. I supposed Julian must have left Strom's in a hurry to get away from the secret police, but where was he now? Perhaps they had caught up with him.

I had noticed Murgh in the camp the day I arrived. She was sitting with a group of women in fatigues, caps and cartridge belts, looking as if she had been there all her life. In due course, she appeared in my cave, wearing an impressive air of military severity and waving another recantation. When I had signed it, she sighed at me in a headmistressy way and said, 'You go home.'

'What do you mean?'

'You go, you go home. If.'

'You mean England?'

'Mean.'

'Can you get me out of the camp?'

'I sleep Fredora.'

'Murgh, where is Julian?'

'Not Julian.'

'You know where he is, don't you, Murgh? Everywhere I go, you're there first.'

'If you go. Then you go home. Not looking Julian. Else stay. Therefore!'

She spoke the last word potently, like an obscenity.

There are many obscenities in the Kuovalan language. If I had stayed long enough, I might have been able to compile a dictionary of them. 'Therefore' is certainly one, as are 'if', 'else' and 'because'. These are words specifically reserved for the demons of their ancient religion, who have their chief shrine hundreds of feet beneath the Communist camp.

The cave of the demons is a large, enclosed space like an orchestra pit, the music provided by a small waterfall that falls on to the stone floor from high up in the cave wall. The stone is porous; the water runs right through it, leaving no trace except a black glossiness. Vala lives in this cave, brooding about the island that is named after him. His personification is a pastel wall-painting twenty feet high, pot-bellied, shark-toothed, night-cap-headed. Around him, bugs and minor demons, even my own poisonous blue butterfly, scowl and flutter.

I know all this because I have been there. Unable to bring myself to accept Murgh's terms, I lost my head one night, seized a burning branch from the fire while the guard slept and tried to escape through a small tunnel at the back of my cave. Murgh came after me and found me there, staring at the underground ruler of the island. She knew then, finally, that it was all right to take me to Julian.

Naturally, he is insane. He no longer speaks, though he laughs sometimes in an angry, puzzled way as he works on his bugproof, computerless programs. The brown Stone Age people of the remote Northern village where he now lives regard him as the incarnation of Vala and bring him bananas and fresh fish every day. I have never found out whether his insanity was brought on by fear of the secret police, or whether it was an innate condition crystallized by the girasol and the demons of Kuovala. If, then, else; who is to reason with madness?

American Fugue

(The punctuation of this story, like the spelling, follows the accepted conventions of modern American prose particularly with regard to the comma (,). The verse on the other hand is of a more traditional type which I hope will be appreciated by admirers of Richard Wilbur and W. D. Snodgrass.)

My name is not Samuel Taylor Coleridge. It is also not Silas Tomken Comberbach a name having the same initials. As a matter of fact unlike most Americans I don't have three names only two but people with three names always sound like murderers to me. How about Lee Harvey Oswald? Or Mark David Chapman? Or John Wilkes Booth come to that? Sirhan Sirhan is a curious exception a man who had only one name and doubled it. No doubt a psychiatrist could explain what connexion if any this had with his crime. As for me for a while back there I didn't have much idea who I was at all but after all the identity crisis is part of the American Way of Life and I am now happily married to my third wife Elsa Hopkins Connolly and living with my second Eva Kohlrabi who also has a third spouse somewhere. Eva is a charming woman with too much blonde hair and a bony little face like that of a cat. Perhaps the feline element explains her affinity for poets. At any rate it must have taken a lot of guts to come winding over the desert in her blue Volkswagen and confront Dean Overbird the way she did. The Dean had of course been aware for some time that I was living on campus with the Veggies (officially Associated Dietary Interest Group) one of the many factions into which the students of Desert Greens University are divided for social and residential purposes. Nevertheless he didn't have much idea who I was either as I had arrived in a simple blue suit with nothing in the pockets and was pretty confused about everything except my art. So Eva took it upon herself to sort him out.

'He is a very distinguished man' she told him 'and he is ill. He won the National Book Award and the Pulitzer Prize for his volume *American Rubai'yat* and has twice been the recipient of Guggenheim Fellowships. At present he is living in Los Angeles with his third wife and their daughter. Except that at present he is nowhere to be found and I have reason to believe he is here.'

It was not clear at first how she traced me. In fact she had run into the Antelope Family a Red Indian Country and Western group whom I in my turn had met somewhere in the desert. I was in such a vague state of mind that the experience of wandering among broken rocks and elaborate cactus trees didn't seem at all out of the way and I remember Ron Antelope standing beside his battered minibus waving a joint and telling me that he'd lived in the desert all his life and couldn't get used to the fact that he wasn't somewhere else. He thought it was the influence of television which is always showing programs about tough cops from New York or Los Angeles. To me on the other hand Ron his pretty red wife who sang harmony the baby the blankets the rhythm section and the vehicle they traveled in were as familiar at that moment as anything I'd ever seen. I doubt if they realized as they ground on toward Wexler Creek how sorry I was to see them go. Ron Ellen and the guys if you read this I want you to know that our meeting meant more than almost anything to me at the time. I still have the blanket you sold me and which kept me warm at night. Also the carved wooden animal which I stared at on later nights when I was living with the Veggies. What is it? I thought at first it was some kind of wild sheep but the legs are too long. I'm afraid your stylistic conventions are strange to me but it gave me something to count as I lay in my sleepingbag watching the living green numbers of the clock and waiting for the muttered whirrs of its unexpected and undesigned electrical storms. The clock belonged to Sandy Lorenzo and he insisted brightly and reasonably as always that it observed total silence whenever he used it. It didn't even tick – there was scarcely anything mechanical in it at all. But he's young and always sleeps so he wouldn't notice. He has no real problems except for being a sort of unofficial PR man and fixer for the Brainchildren (Associated Intellectual Interest Group) on campus.

Nevertheless he is a nice guy and the Veggies are nice girls too. No doubt I would have had a lot of fun in that situation if I could only have known for certain that it was me who was having it. Naturally I could just have picked a name out of the air e.g. James Milliner Hubbard one which seems to go well with my stocky greying bearded appearance as noticed by me in a mirror outside Dean Overbird's office when I was going to be interviewed by him after my existence on campus had finally been taken official note of. But the odds against any name being the right one are literally millions to one so that to pick a name was always in practice to feel an impostor. At night I wrote long lists of names eliminating all of them:

>Aaronovitch
>Abel
>Abrahams
>Abromsky
>Acanthus
>Ackroyd
>Actifed
>etc.

And in Dean Overbird's office we discussed two more – Samuel Taylor Coleridge and Silas Tomken Comberbach. Sitting on rather than in a new leather armchair and surrounded by shiny new books as if his image had just been renovated and perhaps years of grime scraped off his genial surfaces the Dean told me of Silas Tomken Comberbach the alias which the poet Coleridge had assumed when he ran away from Cambridge England and joined the army. Fortunately his erudition displayed itself in his correction of an officer's quotation from Aeschylus and he was sent back where he belonged. Coleridge had been a bad Trooper and had let his musket get rusty. Dean Overbird laughed selfconsciously and his eyes were sad behind a long and tentative nose. In return for this news I explained how Sandy Lorenzo had arranged with Barb and Cheryl the two Veggies who found me sleeping behind a rock and brought me home for purposes of their own that I should be allowed to give poetry readings in the ADIG main recreation hall and that the first of these was planned for next Thursday at 8.30 and then he arranged an appointment for me with the university psychiatrist a man in a small grey suit who seems to be all wrists and teeth and not always the same teeth either as he has a smile that can begin in any area of his mouth and never manages to occupy all of it at once.

'My friend' he told me 'you are in what psychologists call a fugue state.'

A fugue state is a state which characterizes certain types of neurotic crisis a state in which the subject loses his memory and sense of identity and strikes out on the road for a new life. I remarked that the expression seemed to be a contradiction in terms as one is either in a state or running away from it but Dr Jespersen replied that life was essentially paradoxical and that properly speaking a fugue state was something one ran *through* as I had run through part of Southern California and Nevada to get to Desert Greens. He said that I needed intensive therapy which he would be willing to give if I made an appointment with him in two weeks. In the event this has not proved necessary as my second wife Eva Kohlrabi took me to a sanatorium in Blue Mountain which I am glad to say turned out to be of the pingpong rather than the electrotherapy type.

While waiting for this deliverance or any deliverance there was nothing much to do except eat stewed pulses and brown rice marvel at the changes that had taken place in the university system since my day (though at that time I wasn't sure I had had one) and enjoy the hospitality of Barb and Cheryl who by virtue of having found me asleep under a boulder one morning when they were walking in the desert looking for edible succulents claimed certain rights in respect of me which I did not immediately find out about as they were a little shy. I lived in one corner of a sort of communal room where there was much coming and going of vegetarian women. Most Veggies seem to be female also tall stringy pleasant to look at. Once though I had a long discussion with a male Veggie a small boy with a big beard who confided that he'd really wanted to be a Wizard (Associated Magical Interest Group (Western)) but his powers of meditation hadn't been strong enough. He'd tried hard to meditate on the Tree of Life but wasn't sure which colors the upper branches were meant to be so kept having to open his eyes and look at the picture again.

'That fucking pink Yesod' he muttered 'that threw me. I thought it was going to be all incense and virgins.' So he found himself among the Veggies where the sex life was assured and the qualifications for acceptance merely dietary.

'I fucked the Qabbalah' he said blasphemously 'you might as well be a Brainchild.'

The motives which Barb and Cheryl had for bringing me back from the desert and installing me in a corner of that thoroughfarelike room were I now realize sexual. One night about a week later I woke from my hardwon sleep to find Cheryl kneeling on my stomach in one of those long Victorian nightgowns with floral decorations on them.

'Hey Joe' she said speculatively (it was as good a name as any) 'want me to do you a favor?'

She undid the zipper of my sleepingbag and started feeling about keeping her eyes questioningly on my face the whole time. After a while she developed a sort of pleased look. Taking up position around the midthigh region she bent over the part that interested her and for the next quarter of an hour I have only the memory of her yellowbrown hair swaying slightly and the white calico shoulders hunched forward and little sucking noises coming from the direction of my loins. That was all she wanted – she left right after and the next night it was Barb who came and did the same thing.

When Sandy came to see me a few days later I asked him about it. Sandy was elected BMOC (Big Man On Campus) last year for the second year running and this year he is going for a unique treble. Perhaps he is trying to compensate for his appearance for he really *looks* like a Brainchild with the blue eyes large head and colorless hair of a twoyearold and an underdeveloped body to match. He has a deep understanding of the complexities of campus life. His campaign for BMOC last year was based on a single letter as his opponents said at the time. Unlike the other *Associated* Groups the Christian Group at Desert Greens was known as *United* (United Christian Interest Group) an appellation which was calculated to make them a privileged faction. Sandy's campaign against it was backed by many of the Christians themselves who felt their title was depriving them of the inalienable right to disagree with each other. The tradition that God's grace washes his whole flock in the lukewarm water of consensus was they felt of fairly recent origin and already moribund.

Anyway when I asked him why Barb and Cheryl felt so strongly about blowjobs he answered that fellatio performed a vital social function on campus. Sexual intercourse is still associated however falsely with notions of pairbonding and the meaningful relationship while a kiss is just something and nothing. Young people today needed a kind of token sex whose meaning would be more diplomatic than passionate.

'For us it's like a kind of peacepipe' he said 'though naturally we have those as well.'

I said I had thought maybe they were suffering from some kind of protein deficiency. Sandy replied that in the strictest etymological sense the vegetarian diet is the only *radical* diet possible. To eat a steak is to exploit it whereas a bean unlike a bull is not a worker but a product. Sandy shows a real sympathy for the ideals of other groups.

At all events these formal greetings for they were little more than that became an increasingly pleasant part of my life on campus and I was gradually able to persuade Cheryl and Barb to let some of the others join in and I found it very restful. It helped me get to sleep when the clock started playing up. And I wrote the girls a poem which I planned to introduce into my show:

POEM

Night falls on campus with its cold
And desert landscapes of despair,
That dark discovery of the old.
Brightness, like Nash's, leaves the air,

And leaves are all that's left the night.
They shake between the vacant blocks
Of faculty. Their springtime blight
Is just the gnawing of the clocks,

Is just that time just won't stand still –
Hold still! You hold me as I lie,
You soothe the stiff revolt of will
And drink my straining demon dry.

All my poems are in the quatrain form. I learned later that I am a Classicist and believe in order craftsmanship and the lasting value of tradition. At the time iambic lines in little blocks of abab cdcd etc. seemed the only facts or artefacts I could be really sure of. They had an absolute individual value as opposed to the relative social value put forward by Eva Kohlrabi in her confrontation with Dean Overbird.

'I need hardly say' she said 'that poetry is one of the oldest and most honorable of all the arts. My second husband's work has been published in leading magazines and journals on both sides of the Atlantic – even in *The Times Literary Supplement*! He has been poetinresidence at the University of the Midwest and has taught creative writing courses in five states.'

Dean Overbird on the defensive against this onslaught sensed the weakness of Eva's position.

'If you'll excuse me Mrs Kohlrabi I fail to see why even if your second husband is as you put it "hiding" on campus I should take any steps to locate him for you. After all what rights do you have in the matter? Assuming you are like most American women in holding husbands consecutively rather than concurrently and without wishing for a moment to interfere in your private life surely it is Mr Kohlrabi you should be holding at the moment.'

'No healthy civilization' she replied urgently 'has existed which did not also have a healthy poetry. Poetry is one of the lynchpins of culture. Surely you Dean Overbird as Dean of Arts and Sciences at this university have some responsibility toward culture. My second husband is part of our heritage. He is a big man in the poetry world and it is my duty to get him back.'

It was dark on campus and people were beginning to gather outside the main recreation hall. Through the window I could see the orange robes of Hare Krishna monks affiliated to AMIG (Eastern) shining a pale anonymous color – notwhite. For the first time in many months I laughed. They were all coming to see Anon the man who wrote those jingly proverbial poems about the Western Wind and that kind of stuff. That was me! Inside the hall looked like before or after a wedding just blank wooden space. Sandy was going round holding an empty blue plastic bong in his left hand and shaking hands with everybody with his right. After a while one of the Veggies thought of opening the main doors and the atmosphere improved a little as the embarrassed groups in their variegated clothing moved in. Soon they were drinking talking and smoking. I moved among the young people and the space around me moved also. I had the feeling that when I had found the right place to stand the show could begin but nobody had told me where it was. Suddenly I heard a voice shout 'Order!' and I knew it was Sandy although I couldn't see him. After some muttering the kids moved back to the edges of the hall leaving Sandy alone in the center.

'You all know me' he said 'I've put on shows for you before and you haven't always liked them. No not all of you. I've put on rock concerts and Classical concerts drama folksong anything I could get. Some of you liked it some of you didn't. Now I've found something I think you'll all like. My friend is going to recite tonight – I won't say my friend Who because he doesn't have a name.' Applause. 'He's going to read some poems which are all he knows. You may think this is just academic and culture and only good for wiping your ass with but they're the only real things in the world for him. He lives for them.'

There was a silence which I thought was bewilderment. Looking round I realized it was respect. They all wished the neat ones the ragged ones the solid ones the desperate ones the devout ones and the agnostic ones that they knew as little as I did. Wouldn't that be something?

The lights went out and the author of *American Rubai'yat* was alone. Then there was a single spotlight on my face and I realized the students had closed in again. They stood or sat in groups of between two and ten close together sometimes intertwined. As I began to recite the spot started to move (one of Sandy's ideas) so that I had to follow it winding among the clustered figures briefly illuminated as part of their heritage passed uttering its dateless words of love and death:

POEM

My cherry's branches hide the streets.
It's mad for love now. Spring *is* so.
I reach upon the shelf for Keats,
Still center of a world I know.

My hair is whiter than before.
My mistresses know less and less.
Blake's shining world I never saw –
I have seen gardens, and success,

But shall not find such trees again,
Though given Homer's sight, or mine
When I was twenty-one. What then
Shall my white brain incarnadine

American Fugue

> When alien rhythms pound the ear?
> The sidewalk's treasures shall be palling,
> My lovelife trudged into the sere,
> The yellow leaf. And poets falling.

There was a disturbing silence. In the loud youthful applause delivered with the feet as well as the hands that followed I noticed that the main door was open again and as one of the bald men in orange clapped me on the back I became aware of a woman I knew but could not remember who walked quickly up to me and introduced me to my audience in a clear nervous voice. Somebody whistled and somebody else said 'His mistresses know more and more' and there was a big laugh. The Dean took my other arm and they walked me carefully out of the hall. As we were leaving brightness and levity descended on its occupants. I heard one boy say 'Never heard of the guy' and others agreed. 'Where in hell do you find these people Sandy?' asked someone and Sandy smiled. That boy is going to make a name for himself some day.

KATHY O'SHAUGHNESSY

On the Threshold

So I got into my car and went. I drove calmly, but I felt peculiar, different, and my heart was beating too fast. Hugging myself to myself like a selfish clam, I was breathing a sparkle of green into the dark – electric and unpleasant.

There was a smell of petrol in the car, and the traffic lights were against me, but nothing mattered. I was thinking of the party, dreaming of flowers in the darkness, dim and pale – in my mind's eye I could see them clearly. They had a fainting, heavy sweetness.

What nonsense, I thought as I turned the corner, what absolute nonsense! I laughed at myself, and my laughing (oh dear) was too enveloping, too fast, and it became nervous.

I laughed while I waited at the red light; then gradually, carefully, calmed down.

And so I arrived in a cloud of scent, feeling the cool silk lining of my jacket against my skin, my bare arms. This was the door of the party, painted a solid, navy blue, and the number was nailed in brass. I pressed the bell. The door opened – a roar of music, voices and laughter! – and light spilled on to the step.

'Come in,' said a man in a dark, discreet suit.

I stepped forward –

'Laura! Wait!'

The sound of my name made me pause: a woman came tumbling out of the party and down the steps with her arms outstretched as if she were stopping traffic. She stood there, looking beautiful and discontented; dressed in black, with fine, hard features.

For a second I thought I was looking in the mirror; then my attention was caught by her shoes. They were mesmerizing: high-heeled, made of snakeskin, and they glittered emerald green.

She smiled at me in an urgent sort of way.

'Laura, wait!' she repeated. 'Don't go in!'

I looked at her as if she were mad.

'I don't even know you,' I said testily.

'You do! We met, we talked, at Richard's last summer.'

I paused to think: and then I remembered. I had gone to a party given by an old friend, Richard Solly, last August. Perhaps I did know her; and as I scrutinized her face (a little rudely), her features began to seem familiar. Perversely, I decided not to admit it.

'No,' I said, smiling politely, 'no, I just can't remember you. I'm terribly sorry – '

'Laura! Laura's my name, the same as yours.'

I was displeased to hear this.

'Your name's Laura too?' I asked.

'Yes. Laura Riding.'

'Ah. My name's Laura Knight.'

We stood, hesitating. The light of the doorway surrounded her like a halo; it lit the edges of her hair, where her brown curls blurred to a rich, indistinct gold. In the shadow I could see her face was older than mine.

'I must go – ' I began again, my voice polite and firm.

'No, no, don't go! I promise you,' she added, twisting the rings on her fingers, with a pressing note of seriousness in her voice, 'you'll regret it if you go in there. You'll fall in love with someone and you'll regret it for a long time. Listen to me: I'm older than you, and' – here her voice became nearly cloying, and her eyes shone with horrible intensity – 'I only have your best interests at heart.'

'What do you mean?' I asked, torn between a powerful curiosity, and a desire to get away (I was beginning to hate her).

'Well,' – she seized me by the hand, and her voice became coaxing and breathy, as if we were two schoolgirls – 'come with me, come round the corner, for just five minutes.'

Like a dumb thing I followed her. She led me down the steps, and round the side of the house, until we came to a wooden door that led to the garden at the back. She carefully undid the latch, opened it, and I followed her through.

And so I found myself in the garden instead of the party.

It was large, lush, and it sloped gently downwards away from the house. The grass had been allowed to grow quite long, and at the far end were two fruit trees, small, bent over, with dense tangled branches. All around was a wooden fence; the flower beds were overrun with bushes and plants and flowers. Although it was dark I could see that the fence was surmounted by a trellis, mostly covered with ivy, and a winding white flower that looked like a starry clematis.

'Look at the clematis! Like stars!' she whispered to me, just as if she could read my thoughts.

'Here,' she continued, 'let's sit here,' and she motioned us both to a bench that was situated in the middle of the lawn. She said nothing for a minute, and the party sounded faintly in the air, like a fairground from a distance. From the bench we had a good view of the tall, sitting-room window where the party was taking place. They hadn't drawn the curtains, and we could see faces moving and talking. I wanted to go in. I resolved to get up and go, but with a determined look this girl took my arm in hers – I wished she hadn't – and fixed me with her eyes.

'Listen,' she said impatiently, 'it all happened to me! You must use your eyes, ears, and intelligence not to let it happen to you.'

'Not let what happen to me?' I said in exasperation; her oblique references were beginning to enrage me.

Her reply was simple: 'An affair, an adulterous affair.'

She paused, and gave a long and indulgent sigh, and then began to tell me her story, with a rapt, distracted look in her eyes, almost as if I wasn't there.

'He was a wonderful man,' she began, heaving another

luxurious sigh, evidently fully at ease, and not at all embarrassed to be speaking of her personal life in this way to a stranger; 'but he came into my life in an odd, mundane way.

'It all began with a toothache, you see, a terrible toothache six years ago. I was awake all night, and next morning my jaw was swollen, and I went straight to the dentist. In the waiting-room I immediately noticed an attractive woman in her early thirties. She made an instant, vivid impression on me. She wore a well-cut suit; her dark hair was neat and glossy, bell-shaped, and it swung fascinatingly when she moved.

'In spite of my aching tooth I couldn't stop looking at her. Even then, in just ten minutes, I felt a desire to know about her life, intimately. Have you ever had that experience?'

I was about to answer, but she was too wrapped up in her story to wait. She continued:

'The dentist gave me an injection and began on my tooth. But the injection hadn't worked, and the pain was excruciating.

'"Stop!" I gasped, in between drilling.

'"Don't be ridiculous," he said sternly, "my injections haven't failed me for ten years."

'He continued, broken by my loud tears and pleas.

'The door opened and the woman from the waiting-room appeared.

'"Excuse me, but I'm finding your patient's cries unbearable. Could you not give her a second injection, just to make sure?"

'Magically, the dentist agreed; and from that moment on, Ruth Fowler – the good angel – and I became friends; within weeks my first powerful curiosity about her life was satisfied. I came to know about it in trivial, daily detail – what her kitchen and bedroom looked like; her work (she was an academic, a social scientist); what kind of life she led with her husband; even what coffee she liked best.

'I thought she was wonderful. Naturally I got to know Charles, her husband. He was a painter: quite as serious, attractive and self-possessed as his wife.

'"What a perfect couple." I thought.

'For some reason they both seemed to like my presence, for they frequently invited me to join them, whether it was to go to the theatre, or to dinner. I was enthralled by them; like an adolescent I think I fell in love with both of them, their life together.

'Gradually my impression of Charles changed. At first he struck me as a distinguished and creative man; then I noticed his incongruous walk. He had a boyish way of walking, with his hands on his hips; almost a cocky swagger. And I realized that in spite of his seriousness, in a childish way he liked to be the centre of attention, male *and* female. At the same time he loved nothing better than to make grave statements, especially about politics.

'"There is absolutely no chance of Labour getting in at the moment," he would say, frowning, with great deliberation, as if it was a highly original point of view. Then he would expound his reasons in a ponderous, weighty voice.

'He was a vain man, and I began to notice other things about him: he didn't like it when Ruth and I got on well, and had a lively conversation of our own. At these times he became peevish, jealous almost. But as I tumbled to Charles's vanity, instead of being repelled, I found myself more and more drawn to him, intoxicated by his presence, his look. In spite of my scruples – for, of course, I felt a great loyalty to Ruth – I sat near him whenever I could, and talked to him constantly. I thought about him all the time, and of course he saw it in my eyes; sometimes I would jokingly suggest we had a drink together, without Ruth, even though I must stress that I was extremely fond of Ruth. How complicated it all was!'

To my ear her voice seemed thick with self-deception. What was I doing sitting in a garden at night with this strange woman? I was her captive audience. I wanted to go, but I couldn't get up –

'You see,' she continued, with a look of cunning on her face, 'I stopped feeling so guilty about Ruth, because I had come to the conclusion that they were *both* quite vain. That was partly why they liked me: I virtually worshipped them.'

'And so one night we came here, Ruth, Charles and I; to a

party in this house, in this very garden.' (She tapped the bench.) 'I remember the three of us stood there, at the end of the garden, next to the small fruit tree.' (She gestured towards the tree down by the fence; even in the darkness I could glimpse the apples hanging on the branches, and the long grass surrounding it.)

'The night was cool, and the party was so hot and crowded that we came outside. There was light from the windows, but down at the end of the garden, by the fruit tree, there was moonlight, a soft, blue-white light, faint and magical.

'We were standing in the moonlight, Ruth, Charles and I, when I felt an overpowering impulse to take Charles's hand, quite flagrantly, with Ruth standing there. I couldn't resist it. Like in a dream, I reached out and took his warm, slightly rough hand in mine. The link between us was instant, electric, and nobody else could see.

'Strangely, Ruth said she wanted to go indoors, quite as if she knew what was going on, and wanted to leave us together. She left.

'Charles put his hands under my hair, on my warm neck, and looked at me, for a long time, with a disturbing half-smile on his face. After a minute I pulled away. But already I felt invaded by a sinking, trembling excitement, and that was it.'

She stopped abruptly.

'Was what?' I asked.

'The beginning of our affair. We had an affair, the most passionate, the most exciting, the most tortured time in my life, lasting for years. But it's over now. I have a child.'

'A child?'

'You're echoing me like a parrot!' she laughed maliciously.

I looked at her in the near-darkness: we were sitting on the bench and I could see her green shoe glittering in the light that fell from the window: so brilliant and emerald it made the illuminated grass look brown.

'So then what?'

'So then what?' (This time she echoed me, but I didn't draw her attention to it.) 'I had the best and worst time. In a way I don't even regret it. But my life was full of unhappiness and betrayal. And you!' Her eyes gleamed.

'What do you mean?'

'You've fallen in love with someone who's in there, who's at the party!'

Ah yes, the party. I'd nearly forgotten about it, but there it was, I could see it through the sitting-room window: faces moving and the sound of voices, a crashing sea of voices and laughter.

'You've fallen in love with someone, haven't you?' she persisted.

'Not really,' I said, uneasy. 'A little, perhaps.'

'Admit it,' she said, smiling now, maternal and ugly-looking; her hair had come loose and it fell in horrible abundance about her shoulders. 'You have, and he's in there.'

I thought for a moment, then said reluctantly:

'I suppose so, I suppose I have.'

'And he has a wife!' she said triumphantly.

'That's true,' I said, and I remembered that green shimmer in the darkness. But then I turned to look at her, and saw with satisfaction all sorts of lines on her face, the marks of age and weariness, spite, jealousy.

'Well,' I said, 'I have to go now.'

The garden was all quiet, with its tangled recessed shadows – and the blurred sound of the party, as if someone had covered it in a blanket. And then she fell away from my vision and I saw flowers in the far corner, dim white flowers, blooming and dreaming like a fever. I knew they would be soft to touch, fragrant and cool. I rose with a smile on my face.

'I must go inside now.'

She held my arm urgently. 'Don't go.'

'Let me go!' I cried brutally, my voice an ugly, distorted echo of hers. I felt a surging hatred for her and before I could stop myself, I had dug my nails into her skin and she let go of me with a cry.

I didn't wait. I left her sitting there and went quickly round to the front door: it was open. I walked into the party with a rapturous smile on my face. I could hear the noise of sinking laughter, and smell the strong musky perfume. And it seemed to me that the lights became brighter, minute by minute: everything looked lit up, dream-like, and I was sure I had been there before.

The Story

1

'I must do something with my life!' said William to himself as he rocked to and fro on the train home, warm and comfortable (sometimes he fell asleep and missed his stop).

William was twenty-seven, with dark hair and a fine Roman nose; his manner, although at times respectful, was often condescending. He was a successful journalist, working on the Home Affairs page of a national newspaper; but right now he was dissatisfied.

It was a dusty summer evening in St Martin's Lane, and William hailed Andrew on the steps of the opera house. They were going to see *Fidelio*. They laughed and Andrew slapped William lightly on the back. It was a beautiful night: above the steeple of St Martins the sky was rosy and faint.

Andrew and William were old friends; at university they had lived in the same house for a year, and each was familiar with the other's idiosyncrasies. Andrew was also a journalist: short and overweight, with trousers that were slightly too long for him, all wrinkled above his shoes.

'Good to see you, Andy,' said William. They drank lager at the bar, then went to their seats.

The story of *Fidelio* struck William as noble and, unexpectedly, the music moved him to tears. He felt a bittersweet pleasure sitting there in the dark: stirred by a yearning feeling, he wanted to do something good with his life, something memorable, wonderful . . . in the same instant he thought of his office, and it seemed a dreary, sickening place.

There was a rustling sound.

'Shhh!' he whispered importantly to the lady behind him, who was noisily eating sweets; after which he returned to his thoughts.

The curtain fell to enthusiastic applause, and as they left William felt in a pensive, melancholy mood. They agreed to have a drink.

The pub was smoky and full of jostling people, talking and laughing loudly. Behind the voices there was the sound of a juke-box song. They found a corner and sat down by a wall covered with eccentric, eighteenth-century prints in frames. They talked about the opera. Andy joked about the ugliness of the singer who played Marcellina, and the size of her bust. William frowned.

'He really has a coarse streak,' he thought. He remembered how moved he had been, and felt superior.

Andy went to collect more drinks and returned with two brimming pint glasses, and white froth on his lip. William looked critically at Andy's chubby, balding figure, his round face – like Friar Tuck, he thought.

'What's up?' said Andrew as he sat down, grinning cannily in the way he had, his eyes screwed up with amusement behind his small, gold-rimmed spectacles.

'Nothing,' said William, smiling impatiently, clicking the nail of his third finger against that of his thumb, making a small, repetitive clip-clip noise, a habit he had. 'I suppose you're happy at work, are you?'

'Yes, pretty much.'

William felt almost pitying: Andy was content to spend his life writing newspaper pieces!

'Time, ladies and gentlemen, time!' boomed the man behind the bar.

Outside the bells of St Martins chimed the hour, and the sound drifted slowly towards the river.

*

The Story

2

That weekend William felt depressed. He lay on his bed and stared at the ceiling. It was an off-white colour, with a few spidery cracks in it, like rivers in a map. William traced them right to the farthest corner and – here he lifted his head to see – down the wall and along to the window.

He slumped back on his pillow and listened: it was a cloudy summer day, warm and dull; he could hear the birds in the silence, a high-pitched monotonous noise outside his window. A car came to a stop: he heard the song on the cassette recorder abruptly cease.

He thought of his friends: what had they all turned into! They had no aspirations. And he, William, was no better. He had dreamed of writing a novel that would change people's lives. He had always wanted to be a writer.

'Why is it that something always stops me from sitting at my desk and getting on with it!' he said to himself, without irony.

Just then the telephone rang. It was a friend, inviting him to a party that night. He agreed to go and when he put down the receiver he felt suddenly cheerful. The sun was out and his room was flushed with colour: the room, and his change of mood, gave him an idea for a story. He went to his desk and began writing.

Two hours later he was very excited.

He had written a small short story. He felt it was a good story, even though the subject was very mundane – it was about walking on a sunny afternoon – very like this sunny afternoon, in fact. Nevertheless he was sure it showed not merely talent, but promise of something more. He would make his mark in the world as a writer – he would show people their own lives in his writings, and above all, he would catch moments like these.

For the window was open and all William could see was the huge beech tree in the wind and the sun, the paler leaves glittering in mystery and beauty. Those great boughs! Green and gold, they rustled and bent in the moving light. William felt a deep peacefulness. Yes, he would write about inexplicable moments like these – although it's true he had tried, and the only words he could find were 'windy', 'sunny', 'mystery'.

He telephoned Andy.

'Andy, it's me, William.'

'What is it?'

'Something very good's happened. I think I've got things worked out. I've written a story – maybe I'll give up work – I'll have to see.'

Andy seemed to understand: his familiar cackle came down the phone.

'That sounds great – listen William, I've got to rush off, someone's at the door. But I'll speak to you tomorrow, OK?'

William said goodbye with a brimming feeling in himself – as if he had only imparted a tenth of what he felt – never mind, he'd do that tomorrow.

3

That night he went to the party.

'So boring, so bloody boring!' he murmured to himself as he locked the door of his Mini and walked down the street to where the party was. He walked with a springy, superior step; he didn't really want to go to this party but Anne, the girl who was giving it, would be offended if he didn't. 'It's the last thing I feel like,' he added to himself, as he pressed the doorbell.

Once inside he drank some wine, said hallo to some friends, but soon, quite accidentally, he began talking to a girl with fair hair and jeans; she was interesting and funny, and he found her attractive. Her name was Louise.

The talk became extremely intense.

They found they shared the same taste in books and music. They both liked going to concerts, and sitting in the front row of the cinema.

They found they disliked the same things: liver and computers.

The Story

A record was put on: it chanced to be her favourite song. They danced together. Without thinking William put her hands in his; she didn't seem to mind. They danced for nearly two hours.

They both couldn't stop smiling.

When it was time to go home they arranged to meet the next day.

Driving home William could think only of Louise. He felt full of a precious happiness, and hopefulness, as if his horizon had suddenly become boundless. The dark streets looked friendly; coming up the steps to his flat he realized he had left his jumper at the party but it just struck him as funny.

William entered his flat and the first thing he saw was his story lying on top of the desk, folded over.

He picked it up and read it.

'What a load of nonsense!' he said, roaring with laughter. He tore it up and threw it in the bin.

A Problematic Tale

Money money money
Makes the world go round

– that's the pathetic ditty I sing to myself, having reached the conclusion that money and happiness have a lot to do with each other. One thing's for sure: my life is a cramped mistake without it.

I live with my wife in Paris in a small, north-facing flat. The rooms are in shadow, painted yellowy-beige, and the windows are difficult to open. It's an oppressive place, and it smells of old cooking.

We've lived in Paris for fifteen years; I can't think why. Day to day life is dull; sometimes I shake myself out of my stupor and say: 'Lawrence! remember you're in Paris! the Seine, Notre Dame, the small beautiful streets,' and for a few seconds I conjure up a seductive picture of Parisian life, like an image in a film, of a fascinating hubbub of people eating in restaurants, walking next to the river: but it quickly fades.

Of course, when I go away it's a different matter. At once Paris takes shape in my mind, and it has a deep charm, and I feel a nostalgic fondness for it; the vast spaces around the grey-green Seine, the view of the Louvre; the bridges with their ornate, severe lamps; the spacious Tuileries gardens. But when I'm back the charm goes, like a mirage that disappears when you get too close.

Unaccountably we continue to live here. Annette and I are English, and Parisians aren't easy to get to know: they're

A Problematic Tale

suspicious of foreigners, although I speak virtually perfect French. The person I like best here, apart from my wife and three-year-old child, is our cleaning lady Marie. She has a nose like a bird's beak, she's slim, with bright eyes and curly black hair, and she has a warm smile. I've come to like that nose of hers; at first I thought it was ugly, but now I think it's pretty, and full of character. In fact I'm so fond of Marie that when she appears at the door I have an impulse to kiss her hallo, but of course it's out of the question. We chat instead, and she asks after my leg, although I broke it five years ago, and it's long since mended. She smiles when she asks, and we both laugh.

However, we've fallen on difficult times financially, and it looks as though we'll have to cut down on Marie's hours. It's a terrible thought! Annette has been saying this for a long time, and she said it again only yesterday.

I was staring out of the window at the rain, it was a grim day, when she came into the study (well, it's the bedroom, but my desk is in there). She had an especially sorrowful expression on her face – her eyebrows were slanting down and outwards and she looked suddenly like a nun who's forgotten to put her habit on.

'Lori,' she said – it's her pet name for me; my real name is Lawrence – 'we must get rid of Marie. We can't afford her.'

'We're not getting rid of Marie,' I argued, for the hundredth time.

'Well, all right,' she conceded, 'we must cut down on her hours then. And Lori, I don't like saying this sort of thing, because I don't usually notice things like this, but she's got a large appetite, and the last time you asked her to stay to lunch, she ate nearly half the fish.'

'Annette!' I cried in despair. My wife was complaining because our cleaner ate some of our fish. What has our life together come to.

'I'm sorry,' she said, and she looked penitent, and somehow more pious and sad than ever; and my heart sank further into my boots.

There's no doubt: lack of money has done terrible things to our relationship. Bills, bills, bills! Sometimes I wake too early, when it's barely light, and I can't get back to sleep again. Beside me is Annette, warm and still, breathing like a child. I want to be asleep like her; instead the gas and electricity bills appear like hallucinations before me: and I can't put them aside, it's as if they've seized my mind and plunged me into a wakeful state. I think about how we'll pay them, what we can cut down on. The bank manager's face appears next in my mind, balding, thin and sepulchral, like an apparition, telling me that we're heavily in debt. I think of all my explanations and arguments, but as a result of this early wakefulness my head aches before the day has even begun.

I work part time in the social science section of the Sorbonne library. It doesn't bring in much money; nor is it interesting. It sounds intellectual – but don't make any mistake about that. The job involves administration: I file information, and sit at the end of a huge, sedate room at a long desk. The atmosphere is hushed, broken by people coughing and the odd whisper. I don't do the interesting work – keeping abreast of what's new in the field, ordering the important texts. A dolt called Lionel does that.

But I only work afternoons there; in the mornings I work on my thesis about human life expectancy. This is my real work and very dear to me, a project I've been involved in for about ten years. It's about the connection between a person's life expectancy and their attitude to life; their 'expectations' from life in the literal and metaphorical sense. It involves an odd kind of research: how people die, why people die, psychosomatic causes, the link between death and depression; and I have made some fascinating, even thrilling findings.

Sometimes I wonder why I've chosen to work on such a morbid subject, but I don't come to any fruitful conclusion. It's plain, though, that Annette has little sympathy for my thesis.

This morning she came in (it was a beautiful morning, fresh

after the rain) with her hair scraped back in that nun-like bun that, if I tell the honest-to-god's truth, I've grown to hate – it acts on me like a violent irritant – and asked me how it was going.

'Fine.' I said brightly.

'Is the end in sight, Lori?' she asked me.

'I can't say, Annette, I just can't say!'

No, the end isn't in sight yet and she knows it. At this she looked gloomy, and I felt guilty, as if my thesis was doing something bad to her. And the fact is, I can't work out the truth for myself. Perhaps it is a bad thing: after all, I could support us better if I was prepared to work full time at the library. But then, surely I have a right to work on my life's project, a thesis that might some day be published. So I stay guilty and confused.

And once again, the root of the problem is money. If we had more money Annette wouldn't resent the fact that I work only part time at the library and we wouldn't be living on top of each other. The whole flat is hardly bigger than a ship's cabin. Our daughter Felicity sleeps in a room the size of a cupboard (pathetic, pathetic sight!). The room is so narrow that her bed only just fits inside, with about a foot to spare; her knees often hit the wall when she gets out of bed.

Felicity is the apple of my eye. I call her Fi-fi, I can't resist it: my little, little Fi-fi – but only in private. Recently Annette made a sour remark about my baby talk (I hadn't realized she was in the room; Fi-fi's chubby arms were round my neck and I was speaking all kinds of nonsense) and since then I call her Felicity in public. That little bundle of ripe gorgeousness! I could eat her all up.

In spite of my democratic views I long to send her to a private school where she'll be cared for and develop her potential. Annette disapproves of this. She's more of a socialist than I am. But I've made my inquiries, and there's a school called the Lycée d'Avignon – very select – I've seen the little girls in their dark green uniforms and hats – such sweet, happy faces! – walking in a neat crocodile down the rue Montparnasse. I want to send Fi-fi there, but it's a fantasy. We could never afford it.

*

All day I've been thinking about my life here – my marriage, which would be fine if we had money, my work, the flat, Fi-fi. And I was just trying to work out a solution, enjoying the afternoon sun, which was pouring in like honey syrup, in long shafts, when I heard Annette's footsteps (none too delicate, I have to say!) down the corridor.

'Lori,' she said, with a strange expression on her face, gesturing to the newspaper she held in her hands, 'do you remember John Danto?'

'Johnny from downstairs?'

'Yes,' she said, her pale eyes looking particularly gimlet-like. She was eyeing me in an odd, knowing, almost triumphant way.

'What are you looking at me like that for?' I said bluntly.

She set her lips in a tight line. 'John Danto is having a show at the Metropolitan Museum of Modern Art in New York. His pictures are selling for about $200,000 apiece.'

I sat in silence; I felt as if someone had punched me in the stomach.

'You witch!' I said faintly. Without realizing it I had risen to my feet and was looking at her with hatred.

'How do you know it's him?' I asked.

'They've got a photograph of him here.'

She showed it to me; yes, it was him.

'Get out of the room,' I said to her.

I sat in a choked, impotent rage until it got dark, and thought about lost opportunities, lost happiness. My mind went over the past like a dog sniffing a scent.

I met Annette at the Sorbonne ten years ago. She was doing a part-time degree in French literature, I was doing a degree in social science. She had long brown hair, and a long nose to match. Oddly enough her nose attracted me, as it was distinguished and aquiline, and it suited her face. She wore old-fashioned floral dresses, and seemed shy. We began talking and quickly discovered that we came from remarkably similar backgrounds. We were both doctor's children, from English villages (Wrexham for her; Botley for me). We'd both gone to the local grammar school, and we both disliked provincial England.

We were entranced by these similarities. I remember thinking, after our very first cup of coffee together: 'Yes, fate meant us to meet!'

It's sometimes hard to believe now, but we got on extremely well. She thought I was an intellectual, with my work, my glasses, my weakness for obscure theories which I expounded at some length to her. She liked my rather formal use of language: she considered it old-fashioned and elegant.

'You speak like someone in a book' she said to me once.

We both disliked trendiness of any description, and we shared a sense of isolation: neither of us had welcoming homes in England, nor did we know many Parisians. She was quick-witted, and sharp-tongued, which I liked. We found a pleasant, cheap, roomy flat in the eleventh arrondissement, and soon we were married.

In the first months of our marriage we took to going to the movies every Wednesday night, eating afterwards at the Brasserie St Quentin. We would discuss the film over dinner; quite often we had different ideas. It was only then I realized that Annette was in some ways very fragile, as sometimes she would get upset when I stuck to my different point of view; yes, she was liable to cry then and there, right in the middle of the restaurant, which made me feel terrible; so often I lied and pretended to agree with her, simply out of consideration for her feelings!

A year later, around the time Annette became discontented, and altogether less attractive as a person, I began my thesis on human life expectancy, and took to working at home in the mornings, and going to the library in the afternoons.

One Saturday we were having a pleasant late lunch when we heard a terrible smashing noise, as if someone next door had taken a hammer and set to in the most awful way. Bang! crash! crash!

'What's that terrible smashing noise?' asked Annette in alarm.
'Perhaps there's a row going on,' I suggested.

We didn't worry about it, but then the noise started again. It sounded like it was coming from down below, so without another word we left our lunch and went downstairs.

Outside in the courtyard we pondered what to do. The noise was from the downstairs flat. Should we knock on the door in case someone was being murdered? Crash! came the noise.

'Here,' Annette hissed, beckoning to me. She was standing by one of the windows that looked into the flat from where the noise came. I went and stood by her and we both craned our necks to look into the room. We made an ignoble spectacle, I have to say.

A bizarre sight met our eyes. A small, bald man, dressed all in black, standing in a room that had no furniture except for a mattress in the corner, was throwing things against a wall. He bent to pick up a plate (there was a pile of plates beside him) and then, like someone throwing the javelin, he put his weight on his back foot, swung his arm behind his shoulder, and chucked the plate against the wall with all his might. Crash! The plate broke into three pieces. He walked straight to the wall, picked up the pieces, and then turned round, enabling us to get a good view of his face, which was ugly, and distorted by a look of sneering dissatisfaction. He put the pieces on the ground, in the middle of the floor, and proceeded to jump up and down on them (he was wearing boots) – thud! – like Rumpelstiltskin in the fairy-tale. What a sight! He looked like a gnome, as he gritted his teeth and concentrated, and jumped up and down.

'Annette,' I whispered, 'let's go. He's obviously mad.'

We tiptoed away like guilty schoolchildren.

'Do you think we should report him?' asked Annette as soon as we were out of earshot.

'Don't be absurd,' I said, scandalized. Annette's face wore a dour, unforgiving look.

Later that night we heard more crockery being smashed. Crash! Crash!

'Poor man,' I said to myself.

I didn't think about him again until one lunchtime when I was leaving for the library. I had just come down the steps and was passing through the courtyard. In the corner was the bald man in black, a small figure bent double over the rubbish bins. What is he doing? I thought. I hesitated, as I was already a little late for the library – but I couldn't resist stepping a little closer.

He was burrowing like a ferret in the rubbish! He had taken the dustbin lid off (there was a shocking smell) and was poking around with a ruler among the orange-peel, milk cartons, crumpled paper. Without a word I went on my way.

Later that week Annette accosted me.

'I've seen him again,' she said accusingly.

'Who?'

I had a premonition that she was going to be unpleasant because she had folded her arms, always a sign.

'The madman. I saw him in the rubbish.'

'Well?'

'What do you mean, well? Lawrence, that man was putting his hands in the rubbish, like a tramp.'

'What he does is his affair.'

Annette remained silent the entire evening, and I realized that she was annoyed with me.

The next day she wouldn't let the subject drop. She wanted to report him to the police: if he was mad he was just as likely to shoot us as he was to smash plates and scavenge rubbish.

Sulk, sulk, sulk. Finally I gave in.

'All right. I refuse to report him, but we'll go and see him. We'll talk to him, find out about him.'

Early on Sunday morning, feeling nervous, we went and knocked on his door. He opened it, still wearing black, diminutive, bald, but with a perfectly amiable expression on his face.

'Bonjour,' I said. 'Nous voulons – '

'You're English, aren't you?' he said in perfect American. Annette's jaw dropped.

'Yes, yes, we are,' I said, smiling over-brightly. 'We're from upstairs actually.'

'Come in.'

We followed him into a large room. All around were paintings that were almost collages; paintings with objects and bits stuck on to them, including bits of crockery, orange-peel, paper, old wrappers. The paintings were three-dimensional. In a flash everything was clear. Ha! ha! I thought to myself. I shot a quick smirking glance at Annette.

'So you're an artist!'

'Yes, that's right. John Danto's the name,' he said, imperceptibly shrugging his shoulders, and grimacing a little; he registered my enthusiasm with surprise. He was stocky; his shoulders were muscly and compact, and his black T-shirt was stretched tight over his torso.

We stayed and had a cup of coffee with him. Annette was frosty, I was expansive. He told us about his work. It wasn't selling well; it was hard for him to make a living. But he believed in mixing the medium of paint, in thickening it with 'things', he explained: broken crockery and rubbish. I nodded understandingly, although the paintings looked hideous.

'Who'd want that in their living room?' I said to myself, looking at one large red painting that had potato peel and a broken bit of plate jutting out.

'Drop in again,' he said in his thick American drawl.

We became quite friendly. In the mornings, when Annette was out teaching and I was at home working, John would often come upstairs, and we'd have a snack together with a cup of strong coffee. He liked coffee to be so strong it was almost a syrup.

Six months later he arrived on my doorstep, staggering under the weight of a huge painting.

'Here,' he said, with a broad smile. 'It's a present for you and Annette.'

It was a large abstract painting, mixing thick green oil-paint with black charcoal scribbles; and sticking up in the centre was a milk carton. Here and there were bits of crockery. I couldn't decipher it at all, but I was touched and grateful.

'I'll hang it up at once in our living room!'

Later Annette came in, shrouded in her grey plastic raincoat, wearing her funny peaked rainhat.

'What is that?' she said in disgust when she saw the picture.

'It's a painting by John. It's a present for both of us.'

Annette sniffed, cocked her head and gazed at it.

'I don't like it.'

Soon after that John left Paris, and at the end of the year we had to leave our flat. We packed twenty packing cases and then filled our car to the brim.

'Annette,' I suddenly remembered. 'The painting! It's still hanging on the wall.'

'We haven't got room,' she said.

'But it was a present.'

'There's no room in the car.' She sounded on the edge of tears. 'I'm not having it.'

Yes, that's what she said. I can hear it now: her voice had the wobbly quality it always has before a bout of crying.

Never mind her tears: *I* have now sat for a day in a state of utter misery, biting my nails, refusing to speak to Annette, with tormenting thoughts running round my mind like ants building a nest.

It is plain to me that had we kept the painting, we could have sold it for a lot of money.

I have a conviction that money, or rather lack of money, is the cause of all my troubles, including the problems of my marriage, which are considerable.

I remember the painting well. I never noticed it when it hung on my wall; now I remember it in specific detail, this curly scribble here, that dark mass of green paint there, the milk carton, the strong line that in some way suggested a woman's body.

I fantasize thus: with the money, Fi-fi could go to private school. We could live somewhere bigger. Annette would leave me in peace to work.

Marie, whose attractive presence really does light up the day for me, could work longer hours; I've even thought of her becoming our live-in housekeeper and cook – a delightful, genuinely cheering idea. And all this would be possible if we hadn't left the painting behind in that thoughtless, invisible moment. And so now my reasoning is plain. I blame all our woes on that one moment. What a fate! One moment shaping so many moments. This notion so troubles me that I've thought of writing a thesis on causal events, determining patterns in life. Annette thinks it would be an unrewarding enterprise, but I'm not so sure.

A Rainy Day

The rain was pouring down.
'Quick, let's get inside.'
'Don't push me!' laughed Leila, breathless as she came through the doorway into the café. A taller figure in a long coat showed close behind her.
'God, I'm all wet.' Leila took her jacket off and then felt the top of her head. 'My hair's soaking.'
They sat down at the wooden tables; the atmosphere was warm and smelled of coffee. The windows were misted up so that in the well-lit room they could hardly see outside; only the dark grey blur of a rainy day. David stretched out his feet.
'I'll get some coffee.' Leila went up and spoke to the boy serving behind the counter. David sat back and watched her stand there, smoothing her wet hair behind her ears. She returned with two cups of coffee, setting them down on the table.
'It's so warm in here,' she said, smiling. Then her expression changed. 'I've got a lecture in ten minutes, you know.'
'So have I. I'm not going.'
'Nor me.'
They sat in silence while they sipped the hot coffee. Their faces were still flushed from outside. David looked around the room, stirring his coffee, a little restless. The café was tiny and held only three long wooden tables. The walls were covered with posters advertising university plays and dances and concerts.
Leila rested her chin in her hand, one elbow on the table. 'Listen to that rain. It's really coming down.'

'Hey, look,' whispered David, bending his head across to hers. 'There's Ann Phillips and that tutor – no, to the left, in the corner.' He grinned and raised his eyebrows. 'They look as if they've been married for years,' he added. 'I suppose they have breakfast here together every morning.'

'You idiot!' whispered Leila back, bright-eyed. 'They've only been together a year. They don't look at all as if they're married.'

David looked superior.

'I'm not talking about how long they've been together, I'm talking about the atmosphere that surrounds them. To me they – '

' – shhhh!' interrupted Leila, nodding her head in the direction of the couple.

' – to me they just have that settled look about them, that's all,' he continued, his voice lowered again.

'And what's wrong with that?' Leila sipped her coffee.

'It's so boring. Can you imagine it? Seeing the same person every day.' David wrinkled his nose. 'Everyone expects to get married as a matter of course. It's predictable.' He paused, and then looked at Leila. 'I bet you do.'

'Of course I don't.' Leila sounded annoyed.

'But you said you did!' said David cruelly.

'When?' She blushed.

'Last Christmas. Christmas Eve to be exact.' David was smiling mischievously now, as if he had caught her out. Leila looked hurt.

'Well, maybe I did, I can't remember.' She shrugged her shoulders but was still blushing, looking down at her coffee. Then she raised her eyes to his. 'As a matter of fact, I don't agree with you,' she added unexpectedly. Her voice was proud. 'I think you're just saying that about marriage because everybody does.'

'Who's everybody?'

'Oh . . . well . . . Mark . . . Paul . . .' Her voice trailed off. Then she said angrily: 'I don't see what's wrong with being in love with the same person for the rest of your life. I don't think it's at all boring.' Her eyes sparkled with annoyance. 'I think you're really clichéd,' she said, with vehement, inarticulate scorn.

They sat in silence for a minute. Outside there was thunder. Then all they could hear was the sound of rain, as the long drops slanted across the window. David looked at Leila: her eyes were intense, her whole face was lit up. It occurred to him that she looked especially pretty when she was indignant like this. An affectionate, protective feeling overcame him as the thunder echoed for the second time outside. He took her hand.

'Here,' he said, on impulse, smiling, feeling oddly happy. He rummaged in his pockets. 'Damn, I can't find it.'

'What is it?'

'Wait a minute . . . ah, here it is. Here, you have it.'

He gave it to her, put it on the flat of her palm. It was a penny with a hole in it.

'Oh thanks,' said Leila, briefly, still hostile; but then she smiled in spite of herself.

They sat and talked, and when they left the warm café the sky had nearly cleared. The streets were wet and the air was fresh. They stood outside and the clock-tower chimed twelve, the end of the morning.

Each time the bell swung deep and melancholy, and the sound carried over the roofs of the town.

Leila kissed David and felt suddenly happier than she had felt for a long time.

David heard the bells and felt a luxurious ache for something, he didn't know what, but he knew he had lost something because he felt like this. He kissed Leila in return and in his mind's eye he watched them kiss. Like an aesthete, from a cold distance, he was moved by what he saw. He would remember their conversation, he thought, and even this kiss.

TOM HARPOLE

The Last of Butch

The envelope felt spongy, it had come from a wet place. The South East Alaska Logger's Association was notifying me, as next of kin, to make arrangements to meet Butch at the Portland Airport in two weeks; the time and flight number, that was all. The high table in the post office was holding me up but the place was too small for all the unanswered questions. I herded myself and this letter full of grim possibilities back up to my Bonner Ridge camp site where I had my one-man two-horse logging camp.

Butch had been felling timber up on some island in South East Alaska. In the four months since he'd left I'd gotten one postcard that said, 'Big Saws, Big Wood, Big Money. See Ya' In The Sun, Bub.' Butch was an element of the forest. I didn't think he could be hurt in the woods.

The airline guy had him in a wheelchair. I was looking all over him for casts or splints as they came up the long hallway from the plane. Butch slurred proudly, 'Rode first class, all the free booze you can ask for. That plane lost money on me.'

'Butch, can you walk?'

'Could when I got on, but I'd only come up with a piss-poor stagger at this point. Oh, Harp, this here's Harry, Harry, my friend Harp. Harry's the nicest damn guy. Harry, will you wheel me out to Harp's pick-up?'

'Glad to, Butch.'

He looked like a sick kid, with a nicotine-stained beard browned by countless cigarettes cantilevered out of his mouth while his hands were busy. He'd lost a lot of weight.

We emerged into the burnt fuel, and machine noises outside the airport. The fumes and high decibels were comfortable. We'd done a lot of logging and living together in these smells and racket.

I half shouted, 'Butch, you really look like shit!'

He cupped his hands and croaked, 'You ought to see it from in here. Well, thanks for your time, Harry.' He tipped him ten bucks and climbed into the pick-up OK. We headed silently south-west towards the Coast Range where Butch had grown up.

Finally, 'Pleurisy, Harp, then after five weeks in the goddam hospital the doctor said it was lung cancer. Terminal case . . .'

I know what a fly feels as a spider sucks out its juices. Butch was still talking but the sounds came past me like cyclists coasting by conversing, the ticking passage left my mind too crowded for thought.

'Half of all doctors graduate in the lower 50 per cent of their class . . . culls all get sent to Alaska . . . doping me and bullshitting themselves . . .'

I asked him to slow down, he'd always been an eloquent and enlightened drunk.

'Butch, how you gonna kick this thing?'

'It's terminal, you know what . . .'

'Bullshit, bullshit, no . . .'

'Harp, listen – watch the road, goddammit – the clichés, and wet eyes and Bibles and bargains are starting for you, I'm done with 'em. They told me a month ago. Indulge yourself, you have to, but I came back here to die. I want it to be a decent time in my life. You'll get used to it, I trust you, once things settle it'll be OK. I could have a couple of months still.'

Willamette valley roads go around the farm grounds instead of through them. The hills and curves in the roads appreciate the valley.

Our destination was the background of the movie in the windshield. We were driving right into the clear cut soothing

The Last of Butch

salve of clouds hiding most of the Coast Range. Butch was slumped back with his head resting over the seat top like a man trying to see from under a blindfold.

'I'm starting to understand how photographers and painters must look at things. Wish I didn't feel so desperate.'

'Are you up for making a stop?'

'Yeah, you still living in your tent?'

'Yeah.'

'Could get crowded, Harp.'

'Not for long . . . oh shit . . . that came out wrong . . . what I mean is . . .' Butch was getting a kick out of me.

'Quit jumping through your ass, we'll both end up neurotic. In fact we need to make a few stops. Better hit the liquor store. How're you fixed for groceries?'

'Plenty of food, but the liquor store should be on the list.'

'Got anything to read up there?'

'Oh, *Playboy*s, *Reader's Digest*s . . .'

'Perfect! Still reading magazines one-handed, huh? Well, those are the two for it.'

We went into one of those two-acre shops that have everything and got a cot, sleeping bag, a lantern, one of those red-handled knives with thirty-eight tools in it, and about a 120 dollar pair of binoculars. Then we stopped at the liquor store and Butch bought forty-eight bottles of Chivas Regal. It was all they had.

'Jesus, Butch, you're really springing.'

'What'm I gonna do, start a savings account?'

'Can I have the knife if anything happens to you?'

'Yer adjusting, Harp, thanks, let's pop one of these Chivas Regals into the clean air and begin the anaesthesia.'

He had been one of those drinkers that stiffened and quickened his pace whenever he was drinking. Now he was slow; seemed stiff and old. We'd got all we needed in town in two stops; but he was breathing hard, loud, and hurting when we were back on the road.

When we got to my camp half an hour later, the sunlight was dimming the way it does in a cloud. It never sets, it's more like the darkness congeals. Butch took in my outfit in a glance. Carbon and Buck were in a corral of rails spiked to trees in about a sixty-foot rectangle. I'd nailed up some pole rafters and corrugated tin that kept their straw bedding dry, and I fed them from a ton or so of hay I had under plastic.

I lit the gas lanterns in the tent. Butch graciously ignored my moving his gear, while Carbon and Buck snuffed at him, welcoming him back. He was whispering back to them, making small hissing, clicking and throaty sounds. When the tent was set up I went out and opened the hood on my pick-up. I always kept cans of chili and soup on my exhaust manifold with hose clamps. I slammed the hood down, said, 'Supper,' and after a couple minutes more of Butch whispering to the horses he came in.

'Chili, huh? That's gonna add to the atmosphere in a while.'

'Be nice to poach a deer.'

'Aw'ya lazy bastard, how'd ya cook him on yer motor?' He was holding his steaming can by the bent half-moon lid. 'You know, someday you'll have to start thinking about eating as something more than a way to make turds.'

I'd been eating engine-heated cans of food for years. I enjoyed the homely spectacle of standing outside the small grocery in Valsetz, clamping cans to my exhaust system.

'How's the job going, Harp?'

'Oh, we just drove by eighty to ninety loads and there's ten to twelve more on up the road. I've got maybe five or six on the ground to skid. Lots of cherry-pickin'. Easy money.'

'Roadside contract?'

'Yeah, but we eyeball the decks and I draw three-quarter scale.'

'So you're flush?'

'Don't owe anybody either. I'd sure enjoy dogging it while the roads dry out.'

The stark sibilant gaslights were too much. I lit candles to help us find each other's hugely black pupils. That Chivas Regal could be habit-forming stuff.

'Harp, we're lucky I'm here.'

'I don't know if "lucky" is the word, but I'm proud you knew to come here.'

'Gonna be covering a lot of new ground.'

'Ultimate trip.'

'It'll be weird at times.'

'Butch, you're one cliché ahead of me, pass the jug.'

Taking a quick pull he wiped his dripping beard and said, 'I want to just die in the woods and let the coyotes and crows and bears and little bugs eat me. Little piles of ant shit.'

He passed the jug and I wondered if I could somehow catch cancer from passing the jug with Butch. I said something about getting way down on the food chain, wondering, and then deciding he was serious.

'I wonder if some goddamn coyote ate my lungs, if he'd get cancer? You know you can skin a coyote and throw it in a chicken coop and the chickens won't eat it. But they'll eat a skinned baboon. Remember old Wade?'

'Never met Wade, how's the story go?' As if the stories about Butch and Wade weren't the stuff of local legend.

'One of the Jesuits at the orphanage told me about a circus in town that was missing a baboon. The priest knew I spent a lot of time walking logging roads and camping in the Coast Range with sort of a Boy Scout outfit. I was sixteen and must've spent eight or nine years in the Coast Range, roaming all summer. Anyway I found the baboon. He was eating blackberries. I picked some mushrooms you can eat, and some wild carrots and showed him an old homestead with an orchard gone wild. We ended up staying in an abandoned camp-trailer some logging outfit left behind. I worked here and there settin' chokers but mostly me and Wade roamed. Spent a year together, more like fourteen to fifteen months. Wade ended up showing me every root, leaf, bug, and fungus you can eat in the Coast Range. Amazingly edible place around here. Came across Sasquatch families twice, but that's some other stories.'

'How'd Wade end up skinned in Leo's chicken coop?' I respected this story and wanted to hear it again.

'Well, you know how Leo limps. He was driving by our trailer and Wade was up on the roof, tearing it off. Leo stopped and banged on the door to tell me, as if I wouldn't know. Wade was just protecting his place. He jumped Leo and in the fight Leo's Achilles heel got bit in half. A fight's a fight, goddammit, but Leo grabbed his .22 and shot Wade fifteen times. All those holes in the hide, and he has it hanging in his front room. The little chicken shit deserves to limp.'

I'd never heard the story about Wade and Leo with so few details. He was detaching himself. We were drunk. I blew out the candles.

It worries me when I should wake up feeling terrible, but don't. I'd just splashed horse water in my face and was reaching for my shirt and glasses when Butch emerged from the tent saying, 'I had a dream that I was winning a foot race and when I broke the tape with my chest I knew in the dream I have lung cancer. What do you make of that?'

'Uh congratulations . . . catching your breath . . . ah, what's the word, oh yeah; *Nexus*, Latin, means obligations or entwinement, or something like that.'

'Ask a simple question . . .'

'Butch, look at this.' I was squatting, with my glasses back on, staring at what proved to be an allegory. He leaned over the tub with one hand holding his forehead and the other on his knee.

The dead mouse floating in the whisky-coloured water looked bird-plump with clenched claws that had left tiny scratchings around and around the water-line scum in the tub.

Butch looked casually at the mouse; then saw all the claw marks. 'Just as well, imagine a ton horse choking to death on a mouse he just sucked up that's too tired to crawl back out of his throat.'

A slice of dawn passed quickly, as it does in a thick forest, right across Butch's back. As he bent over to flick the mouse out of the tub I knew how he'd die. He mused, 'If you were a mouse and had the choice of scratching around a tub and drowning or letting a cat play with you to death, I wonder what you'd do.' I suspect we both recognized the germ.

We'd both dressed for a day's work, the rain that pinged on our tin hats wasn't enough to keep you from starting. I threw the horses a few forkfuls of hay and we listened to the chewing resonance of their huge heads fill the shed. Butch was rolling a cigarette with his elbows on the middle rail, his beard cushioning his chin on the top rail. His white veinous hands looked uprooted. To watch Butch smoke made you want to smoke. It was a ceremony. He was blowing smoke rings up into the rain, unblinking as a burning tree.

Carbon lifted his tail up and sideways, like a quizzical eyebrow, and some blind, white worms suffocated in the streaming air around the turds. He was a good working horse. My failure to stop the worms in him was quenching his black coat. His eyes and virility were still canny and he dominated the gelding Buck, who outweighed him by hundreds of pounds. Butch whispered to Carbon whose ears were searching all around the shed.

'Butch, let's sit in the pick-up and have another cup.'

'Sure, I'll fix the mud while you warm her up.'

When the slight patter of rain falling on your hard hat is suddenly multiplied by the area of the roof of a pick-up it sounds like it's raining about fifty times harder from inside the comfortable cab. We both knew the protocol. Butch climbed in with a Thermos and extra mug.

'Listen to it, Harp, it's starting to pick up momentum.'

'Yeah.'

'You still gonna saw?'

'In between these lashings I could get some stuff down. Might get a little crazy though. Wind's picking up some, too. Isn't it?'

'Sure is. Shoot some pool?'

'Sounds a lot safer. Where?' I was curious about where Butch would show himself.

'Tick's?'

'Yeah, nice tables there.' It was a place loggers wouldn't usually go. The coffee was mostly Chivas. We had a few cups driving down into town.

Suspenders are a great aid to pool table strutting and posing. We drank top-shelf whisky and played a good while.

'Butch, you need to pick up anything?'

'Matter of fact I should spend the rest of the day taking care of some stuff. You mind killin' the afternoon?'

'Where can I drop you off?'

'Court house.'

'They'll love to get their hands on you.'

'It's gonna be expensive, and then some.'

'Are you serious?'

'Dead serious.'

'Sounds grave.'

'You're real close to the truth, Harp.'

We agreed to meet at one of two bars, depending on the time. Just before dark we met at the better of the two. The place usually felt like a playground; good folks, pool tables, big dance floor, and those gambling computers. But they had the lights real bright, for cleaning; scarred chair legs sticking up. We left.

Up in the camp it was cold and foggy. The tent felt as seedy in the lantern lights as the bar had.

'This is a six-man army tent?'

'Yeah.'

'It could sure make six guys ready for a fight.'

'Butch, while you were gone today; well, I sound kind of crass maybe, but I could tell you were serious about the coyotes and crows eating you, and it's high-minded of you, I mean, I admire the idea – I am drunk – but, uh, I've got to finish this job by mid-May and I can't picture myself just ignoring the carrion, or whatever in hell is going to happen.' I was scaring myself. I wanted out, or just to have things stop. I didn't know.

'Aw, Harp, sorry, I know you thought I was serious. You sure look for heroes in weird places. Today things clicked: I have some proper plans and shit started. Money don't talk, it lubricates.'

'OK, I'm cooking up a plan of my own. I'm taking off right now for Bend; go see Caroline.'

'Give her my best. Keys in the stock truck?'

'Yeah, chili and soup on the exhaust.'

'Kinda sudden, ain't it, what if I die while you're gone?'

'What if I kill myself driving 120 miles over the Cascades drunk?'

'See ya, Bub, take care of that gal.'

The road up the South Santiam is a lot like the river it runs along. At night, with no traffic, it was like riding a speedboat. I got to Caroline's workshop at nine o'clock. She was real wound up, working adeptly, but burnt out. She'd made tepees. She'd built fifty-foot long tables where she rolled around forty-five-pound bolts of canvas and she could cut seven layers of canvas at a time.

Butch and I had met her at a horse show. We'd been walking sort of wall-eyed down the middle of some rows of horse trailers, many with horses tied to them and eating hay off tail-gates. When you're amongst horses' asses you notice everything and we both noticed Caroline and this mare struggling for some time. Caroline was easy to look at and we were just hanging around Butch's pick-up. She tried everything that patience and good horsemanship would suggest; and then some. But that mare wouldn't step into her trailer. Butch walked over and offered to help. Caroline said something like she'd 'sell the goddamn mare for five bucks', or worse. She backed off and Butch hooked a finger in the mare's halter and he must have whispered to her for fifteen minutes. Then they walked into the trailer. He came out, secured the door and said, 'There's too many good horses in the world to put up with that mare. She's stupid mean. I'd take cannery price if she was mine.'

Caroline was set back by this whole scene and pronouncement, but cool enough to have a beer with us. Sitting on Butch's tail-gate, slow sunset to watch, we talked about some of the inane idiocy of horse shows. She connected horses to Saturn, but didn't sound too dogmatic about it. Interesting gal. Before she left, the hairs on our arms brushed a few times and we both made promises we'd damn sure keep.

This was the fourth time I'd made the trip over the Cascades to see her.

She set down her scissors and gave me one of those limp new presses that are supposed to pass for hugs.

'Harp, I am absolutely swamped, if it's hormones bringing you over the hills . . . I don't know.'

'Caroline, slow down.'

'That's easy for you to say.'

'Caroline, Butch needs a tepee.'

'I'm booked up for six weeks.'

'He has terminal lung cancer, it's a place for him to live until he dies.'

She sagged over the table, breathing fast and loud, and grabbed handfuls of her thick blonde hair. 'How old?'

'Thirty-eight, goddammit, thirty-eight, and he's dying and it isn't going to stop.' Tears were coming, coming for both of us.

'What a strange, strange cycle.' She sort of choked that out.

'Tight circle.'

'He needs a new tight, white tepee. And an amulet. Can you hang around?'

'Yeah, it's not like an ambulance trip or something.'

Her house was a twelve- by sixteen-foot lofted, magic place. She'd built it herself, without electricity. There were a lot of things in view on shelves, and suspended, and great rugs. She got out a cigar box and took an eagle skull out and plucked tiny feathers from between its eyes. She laid them on a wisp of mountain-goat fur and then used some clay from some famous arch in Greece. She spat on these things and worked the clay with the feathers and fur in it, into a ball, then into a snake shape. Then she pulled out a pink sliver of wood, from a Ponderosa pine that had been struck by lightning and scarred to the ground, but lived. She wound the clay and fur and feathered snake around the sliver, then stuck it into an odd-shaped piece of leather. It was a piece of tanned Percheron scrotum from a stud I had gelded. I forgot I'd given it to her. Before she sewed it shut she handed it to me and said, 'Think about Butch and horse-whispering for a while then spit your tobacco in there.' When it was sewn shut she said, 'That's the kind of sewing I should be doing.'

'Yeah, well, it's all women's work.'

She pointed the long needle of her hand-awl at me, 'Careful, tree-killer.'

'Now, Caroline, you know it's only gardening on a grand scale.'

She was a fun and flexible woman, but a witch is a witch. I mentioned her allusion to hormones. She made a suspicious-smelling herb tea and we talked for hours in her little velvet home. Remorse; she explained things that aligned my mind with Butch. I could sure get a grip on things around her sometimes. We spent a gratifying night, cooked eggs and carried water to her garden in the morning, while I nursed a New-Age mind-hangover into gratitude for good friends. The image of Butch in the foreground, middleground and background of my life was now, somehow acceptable.

Back at her shop she gave me a brand-new eighteen-foot diameter tepee, a gift for Butch. We made promises that weren't nearly as dear as those first electric arm-hair ones.

Hugs should be long bear hugs that leave you with some certainty of the person you are hugging. We hugged. Caroline said in the wake of a sigh, 'Harp, this business, sometimes . . .'

'I'll be back soon, real soon, to spend some time.'

'You'll learn things that'll change everything you know. Pay close attention.' Her eyes were flicking back and forth from one of mine to the other as though she were reading two books at once.

'Well, when this thing's done I'll bring some dynamite over and make you a ten-foot-deep outhouse hole. The Butch Memorial Powder Room.'

'I'll feed you, deal. Be good to yourself. What was that Latin word? *Nexus*?'

'Yeah.' I tend to get a lot of mileage out of words that intrigue me.

'Give Butch my love.'

'He'll know all about it. You're one good woman.'

'You sweet-talker, Harp. Get out of here and go set up that tepee.'

When I got back to camp the stock truck tail-gate was still down. Buck was fed, Carbon and Butch were gone. As I made the twenty tepee poles, the sun on my hands and arms made them look akin to the trees I was working with. Peeling poles that smooth is sculpture. The lightness of the work, my mind, and the day all suggested art forms.

I had erected tepees five or six times using a book that had photographs of a 1950 Studebaker, with tepee poles lashed to it. Things in the '50s had balance and sense. The book was a homely and exact description of a process that would have tempted many a writer to more flowery stuff. Just the facts and bits of folklore.

The Last of Butch

It went up, if I say so myself, perfectly. Big tight white cone. I had remembered to tie a horse-tail flag to the door pole. Buck wouldn't miss it until fly-time. I'd just got a fire going in there, and was settling down as I listened to Carbon and Butch's leave-taking outside.

Butch came in with a painful decorum, but he'd had a good day of riding and foraging with Carbon. He took it in, looking up, down, and around with the fire building and pulsing light on him.

'Man, like the warm inside of a 1950s teat in a tight sweater. Caroline make it?'

'Yeah, gift, she sends her love and this amulet.'

'A tent with a fire inside, those Indians were really on their way.' He was peeling off some layers, it was bright and warm in there.

'How'd you and Carbon do?' I never knew anyone that went on unfettered walks with a horse. The day was mostly up to the horse. Butch would just hang around with him all day. Sometimes sitting on him, unbridled, or standing listening; or eating alongside him.

'Harp, old Carbon has about as much time left as I do.'

'I don't think he's that bad yet.'

'You wish.'

*

We spent most of the next four or five weeks drinking Chivas Regal. I worked a day here and there when Butch went to town. The tepee was the vortex of our meals, drinking, talking; a cone of light and Butch let the little hairy amulet tickle his chest. We spent the days walking and sitting on the stumps of jobs we'd done over the years. New growth was taller than we were on the older clear-cuts. Butch showed me some things that Wade had taught him. It was getting harder for him to get around; he used the binoculars more and I kept the windows on the old Ford real clean. Then it got to the point where I'd make him a sort of sleeping-bag nest and he only got out to piss.

*

It was cold and calm the morning after we finished that last jug of Chivas. I poked my head in Butch's tepee. He looked puny – rolling a cigarette with his white, atrophied arms sticking out of his sleeping-bag. I built a fire and split up a bunch more kindling. 'Krusteaz and cackle berries?'

'Suit yourself, Harp.' Butch dressed and went outside awkwardly. When I finished eating the sun was up, but not warming up yet. He was out whispering to Carbon.

'Goodbye, old man.' I'd never heard him speak to Carbon in English before.

'Goodbye, Harp, there's the inevitable envelope in there under my pillow. Two, in fact.'

'Really, Butch?'

'Well now, I wouldn't sneak away. Don't hug me, Bub, I'd break. Your pick-up will be at Stan's saw shop in Newport.'

The red-handled knife, binoculars, and paperwork were under his pillow. The piece of paper folded in half that said 'Harp' on it said to go to Baboon ridge and dig a grave next to where Wade's bones were buried. It said it would be marked with surveyor's stakes with red ribbons. I was then to proceed, no shit, he wrote 'proceed', to the Yaguina Bay Coast Guard station with the tepee cover.

The grave site, as well as about a sixty-foot circle around it, were clearly staked. I dug his grave and just left the pick and shovel there.

Butch had flicked himself off the bay bridge like a cigarette.

When I got to the Coast Guard they directed me to the coroner's. I introduced myself to him and gave him the envelope. It had three different letters in it. Things felt too mechanical and cold. I just said I'd be back in a while. Coroners must see a weird range

The Last of Butch

of reactions from people, but he hadn't seen anything yet. Butch had been busy on those trips to town. I brought my pick-up back from Stan's. When I got back the coroner was experimenting with facial expressions.

'According to these papers, you are here to claim the body of one John Percival Brim. I am familiar with the law here, but I called the County Attorney and he was actually anticipating my call. This is extraordinary.'

'No shit, 'scuse the French, Doctor. Would you help me wrap him up?' We laid the huge tepee in the hallway and rolled Butch up in it. The doctor was a good help but he was real uncomfortable. It was unbelievable. We loaded him in the front of the pick-up, sitting. I thought about tying him but didn't. The doctor was gone.

Back at Baboon ridge I laid Butch next to the hole and rigged some ropes around him and lowered him. It was terrible, but the dirt falling on the canvas was easier to listen to than what I've heard of dirt hitting coffins.

When I got back from blasting Caroline's outhouse hole I took thirteen spruce saplings, all about three feet tall, and planted them in a circle around the grave and one right on top of Butch, where the ground had sunk a bit.

Old Carbon died two weeks later.

That was fifteen years ago. I went up to Baboon ridge last summer. The tree on Butch was eight or nine feet taller than all the others in the circle. I picked a cone off it, feeling and smelling and looking – wondering where in the cosmos spirals start.

Making a Moose Die

The disinfectant determination of the janitor and the shiny chemical cleanliness of the locker room seemed too plush for the abject losers. Hissing showers echoed hometown reactions and provided steamy anonymity. There was nothing to say and eye contact was nil.

The Fighting Saints football team had just put in the most uniformly puny performance in memory.

Some exaggerated limps and inflamed tissue were blamed on the below-freezing days that had left the formerly spongy field as hard as the parking lot. But, 'Goddammit . . . both teams . . . oh, goddammit . . . played . . . goddammit to hell . . . on the same . . . goddamn, GODDAMMIT . . . surface,' the coach was wont to point out as he kept shoving his false teeth back in his spittle-flinging mouth. No one thought he was cursing his dentures.

Big Al sat on the floor wondering if he could just throw his towel right into the concrete. He wanted to slam something so hard it would disappear or die.

Al had always been the biggest kid in Great Falls and was probably the biggest man in Montana. He loved his 332 pounds and maintained them by lifting weights twice daily, and taking steroids. He liked breaking rocks and boards and other football players.

Today, the second biggest kid in Montana, and probably the trickiest, had made Al look like a fool. Al had never known what a threat to his primitive ego would feel like. He was looking down at his huge white and red and black and blue body thinking about a gorilla he'd seen at a zoo in Denver. The surly

Making a Moose Die

primate would shit in his hand and throw it at the spactators. Al felt caged and wanted to be in the Studebaker with a box of beer in his lap. He liked these new aluminium beer cans. He liked squeezing the beer out of them. But if it was bottles he liked biting the caps off them if someone was watching.

Jay was gliding across the floor near Al like a cat. His feline elegance on the football field seemed to anticipate trouble and shun it, like the way a cat slinks out of a room just before an argument starts.

He was one of two black men in an all-white town; the other being the antiseptic crusader that shined the floor that the team was now moping on. Jay knew he was always watched, he was good at it. He had developed a walk that looked more like swimming insouciantly from the depths of an ocean. He could make shaking salt look choreographed.

Today he'd felt the first joyless dent in his antic disregard for the grunting white boys that usually couldn't stop him. He hadn't been hurt but his cat-spirit was bruised.

'Shee mufuckas we be pokin' the pooch, ain't sellin no pups.'

Kevin's fascination and covert study of Jay's endless obscene repertoire of idiom, metaphor, and hybrid invective, let him catch the drift of his post-game summation.

Having grown up on a farm, Kevin's knowledge of barnyard habitués often gave him a sense of home when he was around the team, but this day had been disastrous. He was worried about his athletic scholarship, which was the only way he could earn his way through pre-veterinary school. He too wanted to get out of town on some back road to feel and smell something different.

On top of all the other bad feelings that the game had stirred in their guts, the three roommates were all aware of their relationship with chicken pot-pies. Kevin, Al and Jay had pooled their food allowances in a mad, if not pragmatic deal, in which the most protein for the dollar was the only consideration. They had acquired, at seven for a dollar, 7,035 chicken pot-pies, with a freezer thrown in on the deal.

There was no proof that these were normal chicken pot-pies, but the butcher assured them that they were so cheap merely because the manufacturer had neglected to label them. The deal was made with handshakes meatier than the pies turned out to be, and all the food money the boys had was spent.

These 7,035 chicken pot-pies contained the edible and other parts of roughly sixty-one chickens. The boys bought them since none of them could cook, and all it was supposed to require to make a meal of these pies was some heat. It wasn't that easy. The edges burned and the middles stayed a flavourless crystalline substance surrounded by a coagulant with some orange and green vegetation in it. Now they just let them thaw and ate them. Chicken pot-pies raw are light but they bind.

After ten weeks of this diet they could control the natural gag-reflex as the varying textures went down their throats. They were stuck with the chicken pot-pies. Unless they could use them as trading stock for other necessities the three could share.

Out in the stadium parking lot was a 1949 Studebaker convertible. They had traded 1,200 chicken pot-pies for this post-war relic with its chrome-plated bullet nose and tank-like appearance. It was about the same colour as the soupy stuff inside the pies, but took longer to warm up. The cloth top was usable but they always left it down, aware of the spectacle they produced sitting shoulder to shoulder in sub-freezing weather.

As the icy gravel rasped underfoot in the dark parking lot the boys agreed they wanted a couple dozen beers apiece. They all wanted to feel about thirteen again.

Kevin knew how to get the drink that they were too young to buy legally. It was risky. The Indians that seemed to live under the railroad docks by the new bridge would take your money, plus the price of a jug of Tokay, that most powerful and cheapest of wines, and they'd go to a bar with you to buy the beer. Sometimes the deals fell through when the Indian simply walked through the bar and out the back door. Tonight Al would be plugging the back door, and the Indian would know that.

A lone Indian, barely able to walk, brought knowing grins or curious stares from the regulars at the Depot Bar. When he slurred his order for three cases of beer and a jug of Tokay all speculation was over about his mission, but the drama was only beginning.

Kevin and Jay were watching through the front window, their obvious concern made round patches of frost on the panes as they whispered explosive encouragements to the unhearing Indian. Al was crouched inconspicuously as his bulk allowed right beside the back door.

The hapless Indian had to move the beer from the premises himself to keep the peace with the bartender. Kevin and Jay watched him try to lift the three cases and it was hopeless. Then he couldn't really handle one six-pack. In an admirable display of good faith that suggested he was going to walk seventy-two beer cans to the door, one at a time, he tried to pull one out of the plastic holder. Failing this he grabbed the familiar wrinkled brown-bagged neck of the Tokay and wove towards the back door. He needed to go out and take a leak and a good long pull on the Tokay and think about things.

Kevin and Jay knew what had to be done. If the Indian walked out of the back door with nothing but the Tokay in his hand, Al wouldn't be gentle. Kevin started the car as Jay slid through the front door. All eyes were on the Indian in his predicament. Then in the fastest and most fluid movement of the day, Jay sprinted the length of the bar, lifted the three cases right over the startled Indian, and he was out of the back door in three wiry bounds that hardly shook the beer.

Most of the customers in the bar knew of him and applauded his deft disappearance. They all knew what was at stake and Jay's gutsy ballet with the beer was a thing of beauty, marred only by the Indian wetting his pants.

When Jay burst out of the back door Al hurled himself out of his dark crouch, afraid of something this fast happening. He wrapped himself around Jay and the beer and picked them both up, with Jay using his invective prowess on Al not to shake up the beer. The topless Studebaker came careening down the rutted alley. Al placed Jay and the beer in the front seat like a baby in a crib and then dove rather theatrically, for a man of his imagination, into the back seat. Kevin gunned the engine and sideswiped every trash can he could to build on the noise, speed, and desperado glee of their deeds. In the red tail-lighted alley Kevin saw a little image in the rear-view mirror of the Indian whooping and waving the jug. They had done the deal to everyone's gratification and satisfied the need for a bit of Saturday night hell-raising. The Indian would be the story-teller with his Tokay mates that night.

The notoriety of the athletes and their car precluded the idea of them cruising around town swilling the contraband. They decided to head a few miles up Rimini Gulch, a drive that would provide ample time to knock off most of the beer and get them back to town stylishly late at any post-game parties.

Their spirits lifted with each drained bottle that flew out of the old convertible. Kevin liked targets for his empties. He'd suck one down quicker just to take a shot at an approaching sign. The glittering amber shards exploding off a billboard took timing and concentration. Al just threw his up as hard as he could. He said if he couldn't hear it break it was one hell of a bottle or one hell of a throw. Jay, settled into his feline repose, just rolled his bottles over the edge of the door. 'Trash, just trash; you niggers be workin' too hard,' was his philosophy of creative littering.

Kevin and Al regarded him with the leers and elation that only people in convertibles with the tops down know. They were brothers in their carefree depredations. They needed this getting loose and loud in the wind and snow and not giving a shit.

Kevin always drove. He'd been operating farm equipment and vehicles since his legs were long enough to reach the pedals. He'd caught up with the county snowplough which was sanding and salting the road. It was safe, but slow going. They needed to pull over to piss. Writing your name in the snow was a tradition that Al could afford to complete in a big way. Kevin gauged his flow and lettering well, but always screwed up dotting the 'i'. Jay, being from Atlanta, was new to this art form, but wasn't to be outdone by these hayseeds. His efforts had become almost calligraphic. As they looked at each other's fleeting autographs praise rained on Jay like pennies on a sidewalk artist.

Back in the car they could see the flashing orange lights of the county road crew heading up Rimini. They thought it a good omen that their chosen route was being made safe for them. The old Studebaker was great on a road like this. Its weight, power and traction all gave a driver confidence on a narrow slick surface. Kevin was feeling heady and showing-off a bit. He was driving too fast. Even for a freshly sanded and salted road.

Around one blind icy curve, with the car barely under control, the headlights tattooed on the boys' brain the image of a 1,300-pound bull moose with antlers that revealed a six-foot spread as he casually lifted his head. He was standing broadside to the car, licking the road salt. The moose felt no threat from the lights narrowing towards him. He'd never seen lights before, and the proximity of the creek prevented him from hearing anything. He knew neither natural predators nor fear. The grains of county salt were his undoing.

Kevin knew he couldn't touch the brakes on the glassy road. There was no room or time to steer around the moose. The bullet nose, with the 6,000-pound car behind it hit the moose in the middle of the back, breaking several thoracic vertebrae and paralysing his hind legs.

The impact, from the time they first saw the moose until he collapsed in front of the car, took about five seconds. Collisions on ice add the element of suspended time to build the terror. The only thing the moose heard was a sustained, high-decibel 'Shiiiiiiiit,' from Jay.

Kevin and Al climbed out over the driver's door not knowing

what to do next. The moose was knocked out, but blowing quick, steaming breaths. The undamaged headlights lent a bizarre illumination to the immense wet beast prone on the white road.

The moose began making noises that sounded like pain and awareness were building in him. His hindquarters were motionless but he began to paw for a toehold with his long front legs. He was getting some strength back.

Jay stepped out of the shadows. He needed to repair some self-image he'd damaged when he'd screamed in the car. He yelled huskily, 'Don't just stand there chokin' the chicken.'

They never wondered later if mercy, metaphor, or simply the word 'chicken' shook them into action.

Al tackled the thrashing front legs and wrapped himself around them as if they would kick him to death if he let go. They would. Jay used his leonine agility, adrenalin and improvisation to get between the huge spatulate antlers and straddle the enormous head. He realized that Kevin had thrown himself across the heaving chest of the creature and was doing something to its throat. 'Hold his head still.'

'I be tryin'.' He jammed his fist in a nostril, 'There's a lot of it.' Jay was trying to use weight and leverage any way he could to keep the head from dislodging him. He was gripping the upper antler and had both feet sliding around on the ice to try for more advantage. It was thrilling. He couldn't believe the size and feel of a moose's nose.

Kevin was clinically probing the moose's throat for the carotid arteries. This was an animal that made its living eating subaquatic plants. He had to deprive its brain of oxygen for at least six minutes. Maybe longer. He felt strangely calm. He'd found the faint pulse of the arteries, but as the pulse began to bound under the pressure from his fingers the moose started to outdo Jay's efforts. Al could feel a perilous and desperate power building in the thick, stinking legs. He realized some difference between the unfettered fury he used in football games and this primordial struggle. He was afraid.

The moose was gaining on them. If he got a leg loose or started to throw his deadly antlers around it wouldn't be anything like a fair fight.

Jay was many generations removed from his African ancestors. But he knew he was doing something important, and doing it properly. He started chanting as naturally as anything he'd ever done. The timeliness, cadence and message of his chant helped them all to focus on the struggle to match the moose. 'Chicken fuckin' pot-pies . . . chicken fuckin' pot-pies . . . chicken fuckin' pot-pies . . . chicken fuckin' pot-pies . . .' They all chanted and strengthened grips and wills.

After some minutes the chanting gave way to clench-jawed curses and adrenalin-sustaining encouragements to each other as the beast weakened. The moose could feel no pain; his hindquarters were no longer his, the heavy growling thing seemed to have become part of his front legs, the live presence on his head was a fading noise, he couldn't know the pressure on his neck was starving his brain to death.

Kevin felt he could hold as long as he had to. He could barely palpate the pulse now. He felt the moose become flaccid and realized the bulk of muscle under the bristling hide.

They all knew the moose was dead at the same time. Nothing was said. Jay wiped his slimed hand on the soft muzzle. Al crouched next to an antler and petted the neck. It had been about ten minutes since they had first seen him stand his ground.

All that was left was to tag him with Kevin's hunting licence, take him home, gut him, and put in the long night cutting and wrapping meat. And, of course, they would need to make room in their freezer.

ANNE ENRIGHT

Smile

The absence of sin makes me nervous. I started not sinning some years ago and, with a predictable withering of self-knowledge, slid into hedonism and the pursuit of The Relationship. It may surprise you to know that while still a sinner, I was much more active. I battled my desires with desperation and delight. At parties I threw up the untainted shade of what I had been drinking, clear purple or amber. It had its own beauty as well as shame. Such privacy was, of course, too delicate to last. Let me make it clear; I never rejected God, but thought the time was right to accept Man, and in that betrayal, of course, lost myself.

Here, you may say, comes the pivot, the story that intuits change, the symbol to swallow. You might perhaps read 'In the spring of 1981 Paris exuded welcome and decay. My suitcase was small.' Or perhaps you would prefer Venice, or even Oslo. Instead, I have two stories to tell and they are not connected.

When I was in fourth class at school, the desks were divided into groups of six. Two of the girls in my group listened to me, and the other two adored Brenda Quinn, who was a superior bitch because her father worked in the army. She had no sense of propriety. Now I myself had little discretion, and in the ensuing struggles, sometimes even the sensible girls ended up laughing at me. It was a wholly moral encounter. Brenda floored me by saying that the birthday present I had given her was a 'hand-me-down' (True but Rude). She also won the victory over our free milk with her daily can of Coke – a substance I pretended to have tasted before. But the thing that made me cry for three hours was that she knew The Facts of Life. I thought she was in possession of the secret that explained everything. There were many things that were confusing at the time, but since I had not yet realized that I was a girl, gender was not one of them. This makes the subsequent explosion all the more puzzling.

Brenda and her toadies were giggling over a book. I never giggled. I was moreover outraged because the pictures were Educational. I told them, 'It's not funny, it's very holy and I bet you've got headlice.' As none of us knew what headlice were, she triumphed once again, and the heap of girls collapsed in outrageous laughter. Her mother, on the other hand, did know what headlice were and since she belonged to a Lower Income Bracket, she took the case to our headmistress, with all the indignation of a woman who has received a class-based slur in an area of great political importance (hygiene). I still bear the mark of that nun's finger on my shoulder. She wrenched me from the classroom, and became strangely energetic as she listed my numerous wickednesses. After twenty minutes she stopped for breath and asked me why I was smiling. Before she had time to tell me to wipe it off my face, or even to give me physical assistance towards that end, I told her, 'Because you are right.' I was dismissed, possibly because I had wet my pants.

I smiled again in Venice last year (it exuded welcome and decay). I was in a church where the magnificent ceilings dripped rich, religious flesh. On the wall was anti-abortion propaganda. In a sequence of photographs; a tiny, perfectly formed, foetus foot, held between thumb and forefinger; a wastepaper bin of small bodies. Also in colour. I had just lost a child six weeks conceived. However, no matter how much you would like it to be, this is not my second story.

My second story is out of the Bible and it ends with some questions. It is the story of Judith (not Salomé). Judith was a beautiful Israelite, a widow, but – rumour has it – a virgin. The fear was that the man who touched her would go mad, but that is all now beyond verification. Israel was at that time besieged by sacrilegious armies whose aim it was to prove that their king was the only god. Out of the starved mountains came Judith, dressed to kill and saying that she had vital information for the enemy. The Bible gives her a handmaid for a chaperone, but we have a more reasonable respect for the tendencies of huge armies to rape non-symbolic women. Judith went alone to facilitate modern doubts about her maidenhead. The Bible says that she went to the general's tent (he was expecting whoopee, for it is a general's duty to add to his own symbolism, just as it is his men's duty to abstain). She plied him with drink, waited until he fell asleep, drew his sword, cut off his head and brought it back to the mountains to lead the subsequent rout. God 1: Sacrilegious Armies Nil.

The parallels are obvious. Judith did not reject God, but thought the time was right to accept Man. She was, after all, flesh and blood, though the subsequent adoration of her people can not have left her unchanged. My questions are these: 1) Was he good in bed? 2) Was she good in bed? 3) Was that why she cut off his head, or would that have happened anyway? 4) In what exact way did the general lose his head or 5) In what exact way did the maiden lose hers? Most importantly 6) How did she view her sin and can symbols forget? My guess is that her first sin was very sweet and very guilty and that the second, as an act of penitence, didn't seem like a sin at all. My guess is that she even smiled.

Felix

Felix, my secret, my angel boy, my dark felicity. Felix: the sibilant hiss of the final x a teasing breath on the tip of the tongue. He was the elixir of my middle years, he was the sharp helix spiralling through my body, the fixer, the healer, the one who feels. But when he was in my arms he was simply breath, an exhalation.

Did he have a precursor? He did, to be sure. There might have been no Felix at all had I not loved, one summer, a certain boy-child in my Tir na nÓg by the sea. Felix was as young as I was that year, the year I first fell asleep, and when he whispered me awake, my life became fierce and terrible. (Look at that tangle of thorns.)

Believe me, I write for no one but myself. Mine is not the kind of crime to be spoken out loud. This, then, is the last, or the penultimate, motion of these fingers that burned alive on the cool desert of his skin. You can always count on a suicide for a clichéd prose style.

I was born in 1935 in Killogue, a small town in the west of Ireland. My father was a small, introverted man of uncertain stock, who ran the pub that faced out on to the town square. My mother died of creeping paralysis in my seventh year, and nothing remains of her in my mind save the image of a woman sitting in the parlour in a perpetual Sunday dress, her throat caught in a stained circle of ancient diamanté and a charm bracelet at her wrist. When they laid her out, again in the same room, with the glass-fronted china cabinet pushed precariously

Felix

against the back wall, I noticed that her 'jewels' had been removed. This sensible, pious figure seemed to have nothing to do with the woman I remembered, and I was suddenly aware that she must have undressed like that every night, unless she wore the diamanté to bed.

My father grew more nervous after my mother's death, his silences grew longer and were punctuated by sudden rushes of speech, always about the harvest or the Inland Revenue, the goings on 'beyant'. He began to sleep over the bar at night, bringing a small iron bed into what had once been a storeroom, and leaving the bedroom that they had shared intact. He became a crusader for the gombeen class, claiming that there was no such thing as good staff to be found. The days were spent in a silent frenzy of suspicion, watching every boy who was brought in to serve behind the bar, until the explosion burst loose and the boy was sacked – for not charging his friends, or shortchanging the regulars, or simply for sloppy work, licking the knife that was used to cut the sandwiches. Meanwhile, I sat outside, squatting on the kerb that faced the square, where I could see over the brow of the hill to the sea beyond. The strand was hidden by a dip in the road, and it looked as though the water came right up to the crest of the hill and joined it in one clean blue line. I ran towards it like a plane taking off, hoping to dive straight in, always disappointed to discover the street below, the untidy line of houses, the sea wall, and then the beach with its load of mothers wrapped up against the cold, children playing in the sand, and the breakers rolling in beyond.

I was nominally attached to a good woman who lived in a rundown house between the hill and the strand; who washed my clothes, fed me and let me go – perhaps because of some old debt she owed my father, perhaps for a small fee. As far as I can remember, I was a brave child. (It is not the loss of innocence that I regret, but the loss of that courage.) I swam in the deep, underwater world of childhood, my limbs playing in the shattered light of the sea. I loved the cold shock, diving off the cliffs, my body growing numb as I prised free the starfish that hid in the crevices, or teased the nervous mouths of translucent sea anemones. I chatted easily and dangerously with the visitors to the town, with a friendliness that came as second nature to the daughter of a publican. Old men with whiskey breath would lift me on to the bar counter, tip the wink to my father for a bag of crisps and call me 'princess'.

It was the summer of my eleventh year. I was grown wild – more reckless in the sea, more brash with the locals and coy with the tourists, who filled the town with their white, bared flesh. My father picked on a young boy called Diarmuid to help behind the bar, some distant relative from Galway with (I can't continue this for much longer) . . . with the black hair and fine, blunt cheekbones of a Connemara man. Daddy gave over the storeroom to house the boy and slept again in his old room, treading carefully and with a sense of unfamiliarity over the wooden boards. His presence there was light, but unsettling. He brought back the ghost of my mother with him.

I must stop. 'Ghost', 'flesh', 'fine, blunt cheekbones', these words are all strangers to me. I am trying to construct a childhood, so I can pick my way through it for clues. 'Felix came *because*' . . . because in the summer of my eleventh year, my father hired a boy called Diarmuid. Any other boy would have done, any other childhood. The secret must be in the style. If I must choose some way of lying to myself, I thought, this might be the most appropriate. Take on the cadences of an old roué in a velvet smoking jacket, cashmere socks, and a degree of barefaced and thoughtful dignity that is not permitted to the rest of mankind. But look at me. I am a woman of fifty-one years of age, in a suburb of Dublin; not exactly sitting with rollers in my hair, but certainly subject to the daily humiliation of coffee-morning conversation and the grocer's indifference. I buy winter coats in Clery's sale. I have a husband. Every year we drive to the same guesthouse in Miltown Malbay. There has been no tragedy in my life, you might say, apart from the ordinary tragedies of life and death that Ireland absorbs, respects and buries, without altering its stride. In my clean, semi-detached house there are only a few sordid clues; my daughter's empty bedroom, a doll without a head, one broken arrow from a boy's bow, that sits like so much junk at the back of the coal house. Where is the poetry in that?

I have always been struck by the incongruous picture of an old woman with a pen in her hand. Is it not slightly obscene, Ms Lessing, to show your life around like that? Of course your neighbours are rich, they respect you, they are proud to have you living nearby. They don't watch you in the street and say, 'Why write about orgasms, when you look like that?'

Middle-aged women write notes to the milkman, not suicide notes. When they die, they do so quietly, out of consideration for their relatives and friends. And then there is the subject of perversion. Old women are never perverts. They may be 'dotty' or 'strange', poor things, they may, and often do, 'suffer from depression', but they emphatically do not feel up boys in public parks. Their lust is a form of maimed vanity, if it exists at all. It is not the great sweeping torment of the poet. It is not love. The only thing we suffer from is the menopause ('Let me tell you something, Iris dear, the change of life is a blessing . . . when he stops . . . you know, wanting things in the middle of the night.' I want I want I want). I want I want I want. I am not an hysteric. I am a woman of ten and a half stone with a very superior brain. I do not know what the word 'maternal' was ever supposed to mean.

So it is back to the smoking jacket and the man with refined hands who translates Baudelaire for a hobby; the man with a bubble of hot poison in his loins and a super-voluptuous flame permanently aglow in his subtle spine, poor fella, may he rest in peace, God bless him. It is back to the summer I fell asleep (in fact a bout of glandular fever) and Diarmuid, who is no lamia, but a man I met in the street the other day, short, fat, his 'Connemara bones' laced with a filigree of hot purple veins. Incidentally, I too have read my Poe and Proust, Keats, Thomas Mann and Mallarmé. Who cares? None of them chased things that were real. My boy-child *was* real – does that mean that I am not a poet? Oh, but I am. I am a poet not quite in curlers, because I make the poets' claim that '*Form . . . ja wesentlich bestrebt ist, das Moralische unter ihr stolzes und unumschranktes Szepter zu beugen.*' You see. In a woman who dresses from Clery's sale, such tactics can only be childish.

The summer when I was eleven was hot, salty and golden. I would come out of the sharp light of the street and into the pub, lean my cheek against the worn dark wood of the bar, and watch Diarmuid. The wood was soaked with the smell of every old hand that had worn it smooth, and Diarmuid smelt of old men too, his clothes saturated with smoke and spilt porter. But under the clothes he smelt alive. My father did not object to my proximity to the boy – he was too busy scrutinizing him for signs of another kind of fall and with it, the excuse to put him back on the train, back to the rocky fields and sour crop of the family farm. But Diarmuid kept his small hands clean. He spoke like an old man to the customers, neither overly familiar nor reserved. He wiped the counter constantly in wide, smooth circles and he rinsed the cloth out every hour. His small body was steady and sure, with the singular grace of a young boy whose limbs have not yet betrayed him into awkwardness. But he knew that he was being watched, and when my father turned away from him, disgusted by his virtue, I would catch the flicking eye and the wild incomprehension of a horse at the start. We never spoke.

It seems to me now, with plenty of adult, if somewhat perfunctory sex behind me, that I did not know what I was feeling then, or even that I was feeling at all. I now know what it is to ache, and how to free that ache by some mechanical means – I am speaking, I suppose, of my husband, of whom it must be said, I became very fond. And you will excuse my tone, I remain prissy about mere sex, though I would go from the coffee-morning euphemism that was conjugation with my husband, straight to the mordant touch and cool, shy eyes of Felix, who recreates in me, and refines beyond endurance, that first passion. Perhaps passion is the wrong word. The sight of Diarmuid made my limbs feel large, as though I were sick. My whole body emptied itself out of my eyes when I looked at him. Objects became strange, and made me clumsy. At night the sheets felt as though they were touching me, and not the other way around.

So one afternoon, with the place deserted, I slid under the flap that guarded the space behind the counter, and I pressed my hot, flat body wordlessly against his. It was a matter of instinct only. The brittle, swollen feeling in my skin broke and melted away. It was several days before we learned how to kiss.

I took some tins from the shelf, poured a can full of new milk into a bottle that had once contained stout, and corked it firmly. I took my blue cotton frock and the red Sunday dress, wrapped the food in them and secured the bundle with my father's best funeral tie. We found our separate ways in the dark to the flat rock that lies fallen at the end of the headland to the north of Killogue. The feelings of the week before seemed very strange as we stood and watched each other. I laid my cardigan in the shelter of the slab of rock and lay down on it. After a silence that went on forever Diarmuid lay down with me.

What do you want? 'The sceptre of his passion'? 'My deep, throbbing heart'? Descriptions of the sexual act always pain me. I am reminded of a book published by a vanity press in the United States, where the hero puts – no, *slides* his hand into 'the cleft of readiness' and finds 'the nub of responsiveness'. And, in fact, that description will do as well as any other. We fooled around, like children. There was no technical consummation, though some pain. We didn't have a clue, you could say. That was all.

Why bother? We all have had our small, fumbling initiations on dirty sofas or canal walks. Why bother to remember, when it is our business to look for the better things in life, and our duty to forget. ('A bunch of baby carrots please, and a pound of potatoes, isn't it a nice day, thank God,' the last words spoken by this atheist, pervert and hopeless cook.) Sentiment is all very well (wedding cake), even large emotions – so long as they are mature (sound of baby's first cry, the look of love in paralysed husband's grateful eyes). But what about passion? Passion *is* the wrong word. I am speaking of the feeling that hits like a blow to the belly in ordinary places. See that woman in a headscarf stop dead on the footpath, her mouth shaping to form a word. But before she remembers what it is, the image is tucked away, the shopping bag is changed from one hand to the other, and she walks on. What kind of images collect in an old woman's head?

My moment of passion was a cold one. I woke up just before the dawn, a white light spreading over the bay turning the sea to a frosted blue, and a shivering in my body that scarcely left me intact. Every organ was outlined with a damp pain and I could sense every muscle and bone. I couldn't feel the ground, or the clothes on my back. I was floating inside my numb skin like the jelly of an oyster, and my shell seemed to have sprouted some extra limbs. They were Diarmuid's. He lay in my arms asleep, and a perfect, empty, blue freedom was all around. The sun had not yet risen. I was already feverish.

School settled over me like a blanket when you are sick. Up at seven, silence till eight, Mass, breakfast, class. I didn't want to speak and there was no room for friends. Instead, I showed off to the nuns as though they were the old men in my father's bar; my hand was permanently up in the air, my poems were read out at assembly.

I was allowed special access to books, and my religion essays were scattered with references to St John of the Cross, Julian of Norwich, even Kierkegaard. You may not think that it is possible, but yes, it is possible to be so clever at sixteen, and then to ignore it. And I was the cleverest of them all. The other girls whispered about escape into town, while I read under the sheets. I thought about Diarmuid, but not for long, there was no relief in it. I decided to become a nun, decided to become a writer, decided finally, to become nothing at all. I lost my faith, in the best male tradition, but did not consider its loss significant. There was something about the nuns that made individual lives seem inconsequential, and I admired them for it. What I wrote, I burned and forgot.

Daddy died the summer I left school – he had only held out for the sake of the fees – and so I was free to turn down my university scholarship, despite Sr Polycarpe's pleading, and three novenas from my English, biology and maths teachers respectively. I took a flat on the Pembroke Road and a secretarial job. I also took a boy from the office home with me one night and woke up to find that he had fallen in love. We got over the embarrassment with a small wedding, me in a blue suit and pillbox hat, a light veil of netting at the front. When we went to France on our honeymoon, I pretended not to speak French. This is why, I suppose, I am plagued with travel sickness and we spend our holidays now on the Irish coast.

My husband is a good man, and I love him, though not in the usual way. By this I mean that he is kindly, not that he is dull – I have learned to find interest in the expected. I should write about my daughter too, I suppose, except that this confessional mode agitates and bores me. Something, somewhere, marked my life out like this. I make up childhoods to try and explain. Nevertheless, I do not change. I gave birth to a daughter and I did not change.

One morning (a writer's lie this, like all other 'realizations'), one morning, it could be said, I looked in the mirror and found that I was middle aged.

Do you understand? I looked in the mirror and found that I was middle aged. The relief was overwhelming. My anonymity was crystallized, my life since Diarmuid was staring me in the face, tepid and blank. Everything had dropped away – *I could do anything now*. What interests me, I thought, is not life, the incidents that fill it, not images or moments, but this central greyness. I saw that I was ready. It was into this greyness that Felix would drop, like a hard little apple into the ripe ground.

Felix was only a small boy that I loved. Will you believe that I did not harm him, that I made him happy? And not only with sweeties. I knew his mother, a proud, vulgar woman, and had shared my pregnancy with her, putting to rest her useless fears about breech births and extra chromosomes. I even (the irony of it!) placed my hand on her tight belly in the seventh month, a gesture that in our semi-detached world belongs to the husband alone. There was the little nugget of Felix, wrapped up in the silt of her body. I sometimes wonder whether I corrupted him then with that touch, whether my voluptas was sent through his transparent limbs, turning them into the clean, radiant flesh that was to possess me before he was fully grown.

In the meantime, I was the woman up the road and my daughter was his friend. They played doctors and nurses on the front porch, I suppose. Recently I dug over their dolls' graveyard. I took some pleasure in their growing, though grazed knees and the simple, sloppy cruelty of children hold little charm for me. Felix was quiet – even then, you could not tell his arrogance, his animal calm, from the shyness of other small boys. In retrospect, he was probably beautiful, and I kissed him often, as children need to be kissed. (Was I a bad mother? Oh no.) When I regret all those wasted caresses, I comfort myself with the fact that I could not have known. Looking at myself as I was, I can only see what those two children saw, a solid, transparent shape that wasn't quite flesh, but 'mother' – the creature that was wrapped about them like certainty.

When gradually things began to change between them, I did not notice that either, and would have found it tedious if I had. My daughter started slamming doors and stealing lipsticks. One afternoon she came home crying and hid up in her bedroom. I was attacking the hall with the vacuum cleaner, hoping that the

Felix

noise would disturb the concentration her self-pity seemed to require, when the knock came at the door. There was Felix on the doorstep, a grown boy, with an indifferently guilty look on his face, and his overlarge hands thrust into his pockets. Little Miss Madam opened her bedroom door and shouted down the stairs, 'You've spoilt everything!'

What a charming scene! I looked at Felix (he smelt of gutting rats and climbing trees) and he looked back at me and laughed with an innocent, evil sense of complicity. That same cold dawn broke over my body and I had to shut the door.

Please believe me, I waited for months. I did not touch him, but carried instead a deep, hard pain in the bowl of my pelvis. I became clumsy again, everything I reached for fell to the floor and the kitchen was a mess of fragments. All that I saw opened up the ache, and I wanted the whole world inside me, with Felix at its centre, like a small, hard pip. His sharp, grey eyes became blank again. Perhaps he was waiting too, though it seemed that when he looked at me, he saw nothing at all. I only had to touch him to become real.

He came to the house one day when she was out. I sat him in the kitchen on the promise of her return. I made a cup of tea and the impudent child held the silence and looked bored, while one knee knocked and rubbed against the table leg. I set down the mug of tea and the Eden-red apple on the table before him and then . . . I leaned over and touched him, in a way that he found surprising.

Small, dirty, strange. Felix's eyes focused on me and it was like falling down a tunnel. He put his hand on my arm, to stop me, or to urge me on, and the pain I carried inside me like a dead child dropped quietly, burning as it went.

Our subterfuges became increasingly intricate, snatching an hour here or there while I pushed my daughter out to hockey practice, piano lessons, even horse riding. Lucky girl. Meanwhile Felix and I pressed out the sour honey of the deepest ecstasy that man or beast has ever known. And while she bounced along on rattle-backed, expensive old nags, while my husband fretted over mislaid returns and his secretary's odour, I wrapped Felix, insensate with pleasure, in the fleshy pulp of my body where he ripened, the hard, sweet gall inside the cactus plant.

Then, of course, she found the letter:

Dear auntie Iris,
Mammy is sick and I can't come today.
        Love
            Felix.
PS Larry Dunne was talking about sex again today enough to make you puke. He says he has been putting it into Lucy down the road but I just had to laugh because he obviously hasn't seen any of that and was just blowing. I nearly said about you but I didn't. Don't worry.

I never throw hysterics. So how could I have reared such an hysterical child? She gave up the riding lessons, the hockey, the piano, and became a large, uncultured lout. She corrupted my boy. She lived at my throat and by the time she left, he had turned into a large, normal young man. He went to discos, he wanted to get into the bank. His mother boasted of his many girlfriends, and complained that they never lasted long. I can imagine why.

I could have killed myself then. I allowed myself to fantasize cancers and car accidents. I should have killed myself even before Felix, but I didn't have a life before, so it was ridiculous to think of throwing it away. Felix made everything possible, including dying, and it is for this that I am grateful, more than for anything else. I lived, of course. For a while I thought of finding a replacement, combing housing estates like a queen bee, waiting for the look of recognition. There was one supporting lead in a school play, but that blank gleam in his eye was only stage fright.

Felix

Recently I discovered their dolls' graveyard; decapitated plastic, split by my spade. There was clay in the artificial hair.

So. Adieu Adieu Adieu. Self-indulgent, I know, but what do you want me to become? My husband's nurse? (Oh, the grateful look in his paralysed eyes.) And then one of the army of widows, with headscarf and shopping bag, who stop in the middle of the street, shake their heads and say 'Someone must have walked over my grave.' Felix.

Felix sitting on my headstone, with an apple in his fist, like he sat at the bottom of the bed, laughing, puzzled, amazed at every inch of me. Felix at that particular point of refinement where wonder, cruelty and hair-trigger skin make even the imaginary and the ridiculous real. He could look at offal, at grass, at the streaks his fingers made on my thigh with the same indifferent glee.

It is easier to die when you have seen your own flesh, for the first time at forty-seven – because dying is a very corporeal act. I don't want to drift away. I want to splatter.

I met him in the local shop one day at the height of it all.

'How's your mamma, Felix, and haven't you grown?,' and he turned to his friends.

'Stupid old bat,' he said. Making up was very sweet, and his tears tasted hot as needles.

Thirst

Miss Manning knew herself. At the age of twenty-one she fell off the back of a motorbike in Spain and a lot of things became clear. Of all the gardens down the length of the road, her roses shone out, and people walking their dogs stopped in surprise. Her gardening gloves were scarred with countless battles, wrestling with the thorn, and they smelt of Miss Manning's life (a small mat to kneel on when the ground was damp). From her Spanish adventure had come distrust, and a politeness that was a touch too vague. Her luck turned. Hems fell, bags burst in the street, and the nurses in casualty welcomed her like a maiden aunt for Sunday tea.

Jesus came into her life very simply one afternoon in the garden, with a small boy who stuck his head through the bars of the gate. He did not smile. He had very blue eyes and thick black eyebrows which moved constantly, making her face thaw a little.

'Floribunda', she told him the type of rosebush, 'because it has so many flowers on the same old stalk.'

'Are you going somewhere?' he said, as she stood up from the small kneeing mat.

'Yes,' she said, 'I'm going home,' and she started to cry.

Every small day was a sacrifice after that, and she sang constantly to move herself along the way. She still had her roses, and grew lilies, did all she could to help the earth praise its maker; and while she knelt, she sang, 'I see His blood upon the rose.' Sometimes when she was singing, she felt him so near, that she just had to lift her arms up into the air, with the muck still on her fingers as a sign to Him not to take her yet – that she was content still with the earth and its smells, and with the feeling in her hands.

On Friday mornings she went into town and stood on her street corner, stopping people all the while and telling them about the Lord. She touched them constantly to let the healing through. Obscenities made her hands shake, and when people showed her their hate, the phrase about going home jumped about madly in her head. Strange languages bubbled up at the back of her throat.

'Proof!' she cried, 'Proof!' until the words boiled over and there she was in the street, shouting signs, with gutturals and labials she had never dreamed of spilling out of her – Witnessing! Witnessing for the Lord.

Miss Manning caught stigmata like she caught one of her ulcers. Every morning for a week, the sheet had been stained with blood. But Miss Manning was through with doctors. Doctors had snatched out all the pieces of her body, one by one, so there was scarcely anything left to bleed. She thought instead how nice it would be if God had chosen to drain her drop by drop so she could pass away in weakness and in light. Her body might fade into the whiteness of the bed until she could float away free.

But one morning, after the ritual of the shower and back to change the sheets, she saw the round, purple disc, a slight discoloration, glow like a new penny in the palm of her hand. A great weakness came over her and she sat on the stained bed and pressed her hands against her face, burying her sight and trying to understand.

'Help me, Jesus.'

When she got up, it was as if the skin of her palms had turned liquid and started to run. Two burning spots on her cheeks brought her over to the mirror where she saw a flush of blood bringing life to her face. When she washed the colour off, quickly, horrified, the life clung on. She felt she looked twenty years old again, like before the Spanish sun and concussion had dried her out.

She caught the bus without her purse, and something of the

look in her large, compassionate eyes made the conductor smile. Standing on her street corner, she caught everyone who passed by and pressed the flesh of her palm into their arms.

'He loves you,' she said, like the chant of a factory girl stamping marks on meat, and they pulled back as though burned.

'I will keep it secret,' she said to herself, and, 'Oh God please, take me soon.'

This is a violent story. The story of Miss Manning and of a young man who buries his face in her hands. He walks towards her street corner, taking snapshots with his eyes. His limbs are skinny and loose, and he swings his right arm dramatically, like a man with a purpose. His face is full of purpose too, but it is clear to those who pass him by that this is the man who God forgot. Who is more evil – this simple woman, secretly bleeding, or the man who walks towards her, his lids clicking open and shut as though someone was trying to steal his eyes? I do not know. The city may be full of men who keep scrapbooks like small, black shrines and who laugh out loud alone in their rooms. I need Miss Manning, because I cannot find the Devil until I have found God – but what of her blasphemous wounds?

Pasted in the young man's book: 'Skinless torso found in wood.' 'Death Cult keeps rotting corpse in flat.'

On Miss Manning's shelf, *The Lives of the Saints*: 'The glorious virgin Triduana of Colosse came with St Regula in or about AD 337, from Constantinople, bearing the relics of St Andrew to Scotland. She was accompanied also by the virgins Cresentia, Potentia and Emeria. Triduana led an Eremetical life, along with Potentia and Emeria, at Rescoby in Forfarshire. But the tyrant Nectanevus, prince of the country, having conceived a violent passion for her, she fled to Dunfallandy in Athol. There, his ministers coming to see her, she said, "What does so great a prince desire of me, a poor virgin dedicated to God?" To which they answered, "He desireth the most excellent beauty of thine eyes, which, if he obtain not, he will surely die." Then the virgin said, "What he seeketh that he shall have," and she plucked out her eyes and skewered them on a thorn and gave them to the ministers saying "Take that which your prince desireth."

'The king, on being informed of this, admired her constancy.'

Miss Manning took the young man home. He said he had nowhere to go. He was quiet and polite and admired her roses. When she looked into his eyes she saw how bright they were, and so she told him the parable of the prodigal son, set the table with her best cloth and poured him tea. They sat in the evening sunlight and he flooded the room with the sad story of his life. When he reached out his arm for the cup, his sleeve pulled back, and Miss Manning could see the white scars of his self-disgust. It took her a moment to realize and then she leaned forward and rested her hand on his wrist.

'Don't do that,' he said, but let her touch him all the same.

'How dreadful, how awful.'

'It wasn't . . . unpleasant.' He smiled quite softly.

'But there was no need.' She was suddenly gay. 'Look at me, I have nothing. I am a lily of the field.' He still did not pull away from her, but under the table, his other hand scrabbled at the cloth. They sat and faced each other for a long time, a kind of joy on each face. There was no clock to tick away the silence, Miss Manning measured time by his pulse and by the scratching of his other hand, out of sight.

'You know that I love you,' she said finally, and she could feel his blood quicken. He laughed solidly, and looked at her mouth.

'But there is someone who loves you even more.'

He pulled away. One of the cups was broken and there was blood on the tablecloth.

'Look at me!' he shouted. 'Look at me! This is my body.' He stood up for her to see.

'Take and eat.'

Miss Manning felt the blood rush from her body in shame and drip quietly from her fingers.

'Here,' she said, and stretched out over the broken tea things on the embroidered Spanish cloth. She felt the song bursting out of her as he tucked away his body and buried his face in the pool of her hands.

'Oh Lord, take me now,' she whispered to the evening sun, as the young man wept. He drank her dry.

Things are made more simple by funerals. After Miss Manning's death the young man sat in the church and tried to suppress a smile. He looked for a long time at the cross, but he had lost his childhood eyes, and all he saw was dead flesh hanging on wood. Under it was her coffin – dead flesh and wood. Quiet and violent as any act of faith.

Seascape

He stood like a young seminarian at the water's edge, refusing to see the bodies that were strewn all around him. His eyes rested on the cool line of the horizon, and sweat gathered in the white creases of his face. His only concessions to the sun were the jumper he had removed, which never left his hand, and the thick boots that stood waiting in the sand behind him. He seemed to be standing quite still, but in fact was edging his feet forward, inch by inch. After a while, a thin film of water pulled at his bare toes, and he leapt back. The jump was awkward, and when he turned to walk back up the beach, he had the loping, twisted stride of an old tramp. He belonged to the street, and not to the sea, because his eyes had that puzzled, childish look, and his mouth was hard.

A woman rose from the sea behind him, the water spilling from her shoulders and hair.

'Daniel!' He stooped to pick up his boots, without turning around, so she ran up the slope after him, her body scattering a wet trail on the sand. The swimsuit she wore was azure blue, with a triangle of viridian at the neck, and her wet blonde hair had a greenish sheen in the strong light.

'Daniel,' she said again, catching up with him, 'are you coming in?'

'Nope.' He still didn't turn around.

'You grunter! You pig!' She shook herself at him like a wet dog and he pulled away from the drops. When she was done, he caught her by the arms and pushed her into the sand, then laughed and walked on. There was a moment's shock before she screamed and scrabbled up again, then charged after him up the beach. The old boots banged together in his hand as he evaded her, but when he reached the towels he turned around and let himself be caught. She pushed him down and sat on his chest.

'You need the wash, you old pig. I should throw you in like a drowned cat.'

'I can't swim.'

'You can't swim? Sure everyone can swim. I'll teach you.'

'Of course I can swim.'

'Liar.' She swung off him.

'You are a liar,' she said, picking up the towel, which was yellow like her hair. 'You're always lying to me.'

He lay on his back, his eyes slits in the glare of the sun. He seemed to be watching the sky. She flicked her body with the towel to get rid of the grit that had lodged in the creases, but he still didn't turn around. The laces of the boots were tangled in his hand and there were sweat marks and the marks of her wet body on his thick, old shirt.

'You like it,' he said and rolled on his belly to watch her. She covered herself with the towel to block his gaze.

'And anyway . . . I don't,' and he rolled back again with a small grunt.

He pursed his mouth. 'Pour us a cup of tea, will you?' It was an old joke.

'Pour it yourself, you bad bastard. You're not in your mother's house now.'

She sat there, for what seemed like a long time, and watched him sprawled damply on the sand. She did not stretch out, ignoring the freak weather with the confidence of one who already had the perfect tan. The colours of her swimsuit brightened in the sun.

After a while, she became aware of someone staring. It was a small child, naked as a cherub. He turned away from her when she looked up, and put his hands up to his face, but continued to watch her through his fingers.

'Hello.' She smiled at him and he ducked away at the sound of her voice.

'Look,' he said, suddenly bold, and with one hand still to his face, he pissed delicately on to the sand.

'Lovely,' she said, at a loss – trying not to give the child a complex.

'No, it's not,' he said, 'it's very bold,' and he ran off as his mother lumbered up after him; 'Come back here and I'll give you a belt!'

'That's the woman for you,' she told Daniel, as she caught the struggling child and trapped his legs in a pair of pants.

'A good, pink-skinned Irish ma with strap marks.'

Daniel lay still.

'Strap marks and stretch marks and Dunne's nighties. A fine hoult for you in the bed at night.' Daniel grunted assent.

'Well, take the old shirt off at least. You look like a maggot under a rock.'

'I look', he said carefully, 'like something the tide washed up.'

Affairs, she thought, should stay in the place where they were conceived, they do not transplant well. He lay on the sand as though it were the gutter, while she turned her patch of towel into a little piece of the Riviera. Her face was drawn with effort.

'All I want', she finally said, with deliberation and a fake smoothness, 'is an intelligent life. You *know* what I mean.' He turned to face her and his eyes were both puzzled and wary.

'No, I don't,' he said, and then as a small concession, 'it was far from intelligence that I was reared.'

'Well, start now,' she said, 'do my back.' He lifted his head and looked along the beach.

'I will not.'

'Pig.'

She flicked out the towel then lay down on it, with her back to him. After a moment's pause he made his way across to her on his belly.

'Here,' he said, taking the plastic bottle of sun oil from its dug-out in the sand. 'What do I do with this?' He spilt some on his fingertips and slapped it on her back, then moved over the skin like a farmer with a new lamb.

'You're done,' and quietly he lifted the hair from the nape of her neck. He stroked the side of her face, until her breathing eased, his eyes still out to sea.

'Did you see the body in the water?'

'Which one?' Her voice was muffled by her arms.

'With the clothes on.'

'No.'

'Floating on its face.'

'No.' Her voice had an edge to it.

'It was badly swelled. The gas brings them up, you know, after nine days.'

'No, I did not see it.'

'Pity.' His hand left her face, and he lay down the length of her. After a while, he seemed to sleep.

The afternoon wore on, and still neither of them moved. There was something obscene about the two forms lying so close together, one fully dressed and curved around the naked limbs of the other. She looked like a tropical fish in a dirty pond, with a bad old pike to protect her. Everyone around them was busy being amazed by the good weather, playing and shouting and soaking up the sun, but these two were not sunbathing or flirting. They were probably not even asleep.

The heat grew less intense, and as a slight breeze pulled at her hair, she stirred and slipped away from the curve of his body. She sat up and stared around her, as though surprised by what she saw, and then she reached for her bag and started to search around in it. She produced a bundle of postcards and a pen, and shuffled through them to find the right one. It was a picture of a cat in a window, reaching for the blind above her, with the sign 'Guinness is good for you' posted on the wall outside.

Dear Fiona, (she wrote) the weather is glorious. The lump is being lumpish, haven't seduced him into the sea as yet. Will you check the cat for me? Should never have trusted her with that couple downstairs. We miss ickle pussums, we does, and you too.

She tore it up and took out a fresh one; this had a picture of a donkey and a red-headed girl with a turf creel in her arms.

Dear Fiona, is he psychotic or what? The nights are, as always, amazing, but the weather doesn't seem to suit his sensitive skin. Besides, he keeps on sneaking downstairs to make dubious phone calls. I don't care about An Other Woman . . . maybe, but I keep fantasizing that he's got a kid salted away somewhere. If you see Timmy, say I'm fine, i.e. give him a crack in the gob and tell him I'm sorry. All is . . .

She had run out of space and was writing where the address should go. The breeze had brought up the hairs on her arms, and she paused for a moment to examine them. Then she started to write on the front of the card, over the donkey's face:

I have lovely arms. Not that it makes any difference.

and she abandoned everything where it was and ran off down the strand, into the sea.
 She could swim for hours. The water was beautiful, despite the cold, and she aimed straight for the horizon. She felt like diving down, wriggling out of the swimsuit and swimming on and on. The foolish picture of its limp blue and green washed up on the beach drifted into her mind. They might even accuse Daniel of the crime.
 She took a breath, grabbed her knees to her chest and bobbed face down on the surface of the water. Slowly, as she ran out of breath, her muscles eased. She blew what was left in her lungs out in an explosion of bubbles, then shot up into the air and took

breath. No. She would not be angry. Anger did not suit her. She would carry around instead the chic pain of an independent woman – the woman who did not whinge or demand, or get fat on children.

'I like independent women,' he had said once.

'Bloody sure you do,' she answered. 'They're not allowed to complain.'

The shadows had grown harsher and longer by the time she got out of the water, her hands numb and her legs stiff with the cold. She made her way up the slope heavily, shaking her fingers in front of her. Long before she reached their place, she saw that Daniel had gone. The postcard she had written and left was torn up like the first, the pieces scattered and half-buried in the sand. Among them was his discarded shirt, and a pair of trousers lay broken-limbed and empty on her yellow towel. She yanked at the towel to clear it of debris and the bundle of postcards flew up into the air. Moving slowly, and shivering with the cold she went to each one in turn and picked it up. Daniel had written on the face of them all.

The first was a pictue of a Charollais cow on the cliffs of Moher. The sky was a hazy mauve, and the cow, which was right on the edge of the cliff, stared seductively at the viewer. Across the line of the sky he had written, 'A Rathmines Madonna Dreams of The Intelligent Life.' The next was a glossy reproduction of the beach in front of her, the colours artificially bright. Along the curve of the strand were the words, 'Yes, the nights are amazing, but as yet, I have no child.' She stared at it for a long time, and looked around to see where Daniel could be, before picking up the next one. It had an oul fella sitting in a pub, the light bouncing off the polished surface of the bar counter and a fresh, new pint in the shaft of the sun. There was a crudely drawn balloon coming out of the old man's mouth with the words: 'What *is* the difference between a pair of arms?' Finally, there was the beach again, though this time there were footprints drawn along the strand, enormously out of proportion, and a figure in the sea with HELP!

coming from it. The caption read, 'O Mary mo chree, I am afraid that the water will claim me back again.'

'All washed up.' The voice came from directly above her, and she gave a start. When she looked up he was there, perfectly dry. He was wearing a pair of navy high-waisted swimming trunks. His body was white as wax and his front was sticky with hair. She was ashamed to look at this body and so looked at his face.

'Oh all right,' she said, and wanted to turn off the sun like a lamp, so they could make love on the beach.

HUGO HAMILTON

The Supremacy of Grief

One eye is half shut while the other is open. So we don't know whether it's drunkenness or whether he is looking out with deep anger. He hasn't said a word for a while. His arms and legs are limp, restrained by the shape of the armchair from falling to the floor. We don't know whether he is about to fall asleep or whether he will soon begin to mutter or talk, or even shout. Whether he might say something terribly funny or terribly tragic or whether he is building up a general resentment and hostility to all around him. One eye is ajar, but the other is fully open looking across the room at the opposite wall. Anyone looking at his eyes might draw upon himself the full force that lies behind them.

He's had a lot to drink of course. Not without reason. His wife Sarah died only three days ago. Even at the funeral, he was unpredictable, showing little sign of emotion and listening to the many semi-sincere condolences either with too much interest or an obvious lack of it. He looked at people's shoes. At the graveside, he nudged his brother to point out the extraordinary hat which one of Sarah's relatives wore. 'Would you ever look at that hat, for Christ sake,' he said almost for everyone to hear. And later in the day, there was the row with the same brother for turning his wife's funeral into a party. 'It's just an excuse for a party. Have you forgotten that my wife has just died?' The outburst was enough to return a degree of solemnity to the gathering at the house and to remind everyone that nobody had more right than he to find solace in laughter. That all mirth was at his discretion.

The next day it was decided that he should spend a few days in Dublin. Nobody knows when the real grief sets in. Nobody knows what a man alone in his grief might do. They had no children and it was considered better or safer for him to be in company for a while longer.

At his own almost inaudible instructions, his two sisters Grainne and Marita had gone through Sarah's possessions sharing what clothes and jewellery they could use and arranging for the rest to be disposed of so that no trace of his wife except the wedding photo and the well-kept gardens would remain on his return. Then he was brought to Dublin in the car, stopping frequently for drinks to hold back the emptiness. Arriving well after seven in the evening, he began to embrace and kiss everyone excessively saying, 'What a feckin' life?' 'What a shagging life, eh?'; to which nobody knew how to respond, not knowing whether he was serious or not, other than to hand him a further gin and tonic and direct him to the armchair where he has been ever since. The drink is on a small table beside him, virtually untouched.

His two sisters sit on the sofa together discussing the details of the funeral with their cousin Deirdre who had been unable to attend. They throw occasional glances over at Damien in the armchair. Grainne or Auntie Grainne has just shifted her position in order to cross her legs and feeling the renewed comfort in her muscles, continues to describe the funeral. 'It was magnificent.' To emphasize, she shakes her head very slowly while looking earnestly into the listener's eyes.

The two children in the house keep running from the kitchen into the sitting room and back. At one point, they stop to look at Uncle Damien's watch. Without altering the one-and-a-half ratio in his eyes, he smiles at them and urges them to try the watch on themselves. One of them walks around proudly with the large watch while the other clamours to have a go. They are wearing their best dresses with ribbons at the back. Their father Paul, who sits on the other side of the fireplace, tells them to give the watch back before they break it. In doing this, they giggle because Uncle Damien makes it difficult by spreading his fingers out. The girls look intensely at the tufts of hair on his fingers and along the side of his hand. They look at his buttons, his face and his ears. They soon disappear again into the kitchen where their mother is cooking.

Uncle Damien looks at a large drink stain below Paul's chair without seeing it. He stares at the two objects on the mantelpiece without absorbing them. The miniature wooden snake emerging from a basket and the brass tortoise which can be used as an ashtray.

Auntie Grainne has just glanced at Uncle Damien and turns to Paul.

'Paul, you haven't told Damien about your new job.' Turning to Damien, she repeats the catalyst. 'Did you know that Paul had a fantastic new job?'

'Yah bugger!' Uncle Damien looks over at Paul. 'Well, congratulations. I always knew you were marked out for it.'

Paul is like most people. He talks about his job. He prefers to talk about anything but Uncle Damien's wife. He doesn't want to stir the heavy sediment of grief. His conversation ignores the most prominent issue on Uncle Damien's mind. The two sisters on the couch have also been avoiding any mention of Sarah. They don't talk about her face. They don't talk about her things. They won't quote her. They won't mention her absence or her former presence. It is almost as if Sarah was a very bad woman.

Every time the children open the door of the sitting room, a faint smell of soup comes in with them from the kitchen. The smell is foreign.

Uncle Damien's mouth is sealed. It looks as though he is about to make a very serious observation. It also looks as though he is about to say something very funny. When the children interrupt to look at his watch again, he continues to look at Paul without listening. He waits for a moment and turns to the girls.

'I want you to do something for me. Will you go in to your mummy and tell her that if it's not duck à l'orange, I'm not eating it. Duck à l'orange, have you got that?'

Uncle Damien looks at them seriously. His speech is slow and deliberate. The children repeat 'Duck à l'orange' and run away into the kitchen from where the vague smell of soup or food is impossible to identify. A pleasant irritant.

The two sisters, Auntie Grainne and Auntie Marita are both angled slightly towards Deirdre who is telling them about a recent burglary at her house. Above the mantelpiece hangs a painted picture of a boat leaning to one side on a strand, the tide having receded far away into the distance. Behind Uncle Damien there are green plants, bushy ferns and drooping stalks; enough for him to hide in thick undergrowth if he were to move back. The curtains are a mass of falling leaves.

Uncle Damien moves forward to speak to Paul without emphasis, much in the same way as he might talk about something he read in the paper.

'Do you know that I had a very, very beautiful wife called Sarah?'

Paul is surprised at the words. Uncle Damien is looking at him and the pause demands a response. Paul searches and rejects all the possible answers. 'She was indeed!' or 'She must have been!' or 'No doubt about it!' After a moment, when it's almost too late, Paul says: 'I think everybody knows that.'

'Do you think so really?' Uncle Damien preserves the equilibrium between a joke and something very serious on his face. It seems as though he doesn't need to blink.

In an effort to punctuate the conversation, Paul adds 'Definitely.' But Uncle Damien continues. Reflective.

'There's only one serious regret that I have.' He pauses again.

'There's something I should have told her. I always wanted to tell her, even as far back as ten years ago. I kept meaning to tell her about it but I always stopped myself when the moment came. I thought I would save her the trouble.

'Do you know that even on her deathbed, I had a great urge to tell her everything but I just couldn't. And now it's too late. It's the one thing that kills me.'

Paul wants to ask him what it was but won't let himself. He

doesn't want to appear inquisitive. He expects Uncle Damien to tell him anyway. But the children rush in the door saying, 'She said you're very, very bold. You have to come in for your dinner now.'

'Is it Duck à l'orange? If it isn't, I'm not eating.'

'Come in for your dinner,' they shout.

'I can't! I'm stuck in this chair. You're going to have to pull me out.'

His left eye still remains half shut. His arms are still limp along the armrests. The girls make an effort to pull them but they only make him look heavier and sleepier.

'Look, girls, stop friggin' about. One of you pull this arm and you pull the other.'

Paul stands up and waits by the door, smiling at the effort his daughters need to extract Uncle Damien from the chair. With a little more success, they manage to pull him forward. They believe that their own strength has achieved this and pull even harder.

'Come on, girls, you'll have to do better than that,' Uncle Damien says. They pull again and he moves forward a little more. But instead of standing up, he begins to sink deliberately and heavily to his knees and when they keep pulling, he finally collapses on to his back on the floor. The older of the girls says, 'Oh no,' and giggles.

They try to pull him up again but Uncle Damien is playing dead. One eye is still half open but the other is completely shut now. Paul discovers by looking at his head why Uncle Damien always carries a half-funny, half-serious expression. It's the shape of the head. It's still a schoolboy's head.

Dara has come in from the kitchen to tell everyone to sit down for dinner. When she finds Uncle Damien on the floor, she laughs and says, 'Uncle Damien, come on now, time for dinner.' One of the children lets go of an arm which falls loosely to the floor.

Aunt Marita gets up from the sofa followed by the others. Deirdre walks straight out to go to the bathroom. Aunt Marita begins to talk to Damien like a schoolboy.

'Damien, what are you doing on the floor. Up you get now, Dinner's ready.'

But Uncle Damien seems to ignore everyone and continues to play dead. Nobody believes him. Everybody is sure he's only putting it on. Even though he looks completely lifeless, they know he's alive. With one eye half open and his mouth slightly open, he looks dead. Dead people generally look like they're grinning underneath. Aunt Marita doesn't like it. It's beneath his dignity to act dead like that. She reaches down and begins to pull at his arm.

'Come on, Damien, up you get now. You're keeping everybody waiting.'

Dara joins in and begins to pull at the other arm saying, 'The food is going cold.' But Uncle Damien even ignores this plea for courtesy and remains lifeless with his dead man's grin. Aunt Marita almost stumbles with the effort. 'Damien, you're too heavy,' she says. They manage to pull his shoulders up but his head falls back and his Adam's apple is pointing at the ceiling.

Nobody knows the difference between a dead man and a man who wants to play dead. They look the same. Perhaps they also feel the same. Nobody knows the difference between a dead man and a man whose wife is dead and who himself is acting dead.

The two women pull energetically. They have given up pleading with Uncle Damien and have begun to plead with Paul to help them. Paul declines and remains at the door with one hand in his pocket. He doesn't want to help a man who doesn't want help. If he were to join in, it would make Uncle Damien look helpless. Uncle Damien only wants to appear helpless.

Auntie Marita is breathless. Everybody is now concerned with getting Uncle Damien up. His half-closed eye still stares up at nothing. The more they pull the heavier he seems to get. They have stopped depending on Uncle Damien's own strength and demand help from Paul. Dara looks up at Paul seriously.

'Paul, come on now. All the food is going cold. Give us a hand.'

Paul capitulates under this renewed pressure and goes over to join in. But as he takes hold of Uncle Damien's wrist and begins to pull slowly, the eyes open wide and look straight up at Paul. We don't know whether the eyes are opened in anger or in disbelief. Whether he opened them to see something or say something. To perceive or transmit. Whether they are open to find out if he's alive or whether to tell Paul that there was never any doubt about it. Paul immediately releases his hold on the wrist and steps back. Uncle Damien gets up of his own accord.

As they walk in to take their places at the table, the thought of food makes them forget. Nobody remembers what Uncle Damien looks like dead.

The Compound Assembly of E. Richter

Frank Murray woke up to the sound of hammering. He half hoped that the noise would abate or that sleep would win back its grip. But the window was open and the noise persisted. It quickly distinguished itself from any other sound as that of scaffolding. The enclosed courtyard amplified it. Even though Frank was on the fourth floor it seemed as if they were erecting scaffolding right outside his window. In Germany, nobody sleeps during the day. Even those who work at night lie in bed at their own peril in the morning.

He tried to shut the window without getting up. From his bed, or his mattress on the floor, he reached up and pushed on the frame with his fingers. He caught sight of the workmen in grey and blue overalls. They were further away than he thought. They were working on the opposite face of the courtyard. It wasn't enough to close out the noise and he had to reach further to lock the handle. In doing this, his body became uncovered. The duvet only covered half his thighs, breaking the nocturnal spell of warmth. His naked body, like sensitive photographic paper, had been exposed to daylight. He locked the window and drew himself back under the duvet. It turned steel into rubber.

He couldn't sleep again. He coiled his knees up and held his shoulders with his hands. The sound still penetrated the window. He stretched his legs and found both the bed and duvet were too short. It was useless. He resolved to get up.

Frank rehearsed the next ten minutes of the day in his mind. Going to the shop next door to buy some rolls and apricot jam. Opening the door of the apartment. Descending the stairs.

Seeing the rows of mailboxes which faced him on the way down, each with its metal door and small glass window through which he might see a letter from home but which more often turned out to be circulars and postal advertising which he then regularly stuck into somebody else's letter box. Seeing that many of the metal doors had been prised open by owners who'd lost their keys. Checking with his longest fingers to make sure there wasn't a letter from home which, whenever one did arrive, he kept unopened in his pocket for hours, sometimes even till evening when he would find a secluded pub where he could read and slowly get drunk with his letter. Cautiously removing his fingers from under the sharp metal door. Emerging out into the courtyard where the climate is thick with work, shouts, commands, hammering and where German workers belittle each other with diligence. Seeing how far they had got with the scaffolding. Walking through the outer door into the street. Lifing one jar of apricot jam but then replacing it again in preference for another brand.

On his way back from the shop carrying a white plastic bag, Frank saw a woman's back beside the mailboxes. She had just locked her metal door and begun to turn around. He had seen her before in the same position. She was always locking her letter box. The stairs were ahead of him. The rise between the third and fourth step bore a warning. *Vorsicht!* On Tuesdays, the stairs are freshly polished. On Tuesdays, the climate indoors is clean but highly slippery.

With one foot already flung into the first part of his ascent, Frank pronounced the obliged greeting clearly. *Guten Morgen!* It was addressed at the woman's back and seemed to rebound off her shoulders. It came back abbreviated. *Morgen!*

His feet had already passed the warning sign, entering the second phase of ascent, taking steps in doubles. The plastic bag with apricot jam and rolls swung forward in counterbalance. His left foot had just pushed off the step when she addressed him again from below.

'*Sind Sie der Herr der so schön die Flöte spielt?*' He stopped and his left foot recanted. He turned and made a quick translation: – Are you the gentleman who so lovely the flute plays? He brought back the other foot to the step below and fumbled an answer. *Ja!* It was always a pleasure to hear comments about his music. It was always a compliment to be asked about his nationality. It was good to be Irish in Germany. As long as they didn't want to know about Northern Ireland or the EEh-Er-Ah (IRA). As long as they stuck to music or the cliffs of Moher or smoked salmon or Heinrich Böll or donkeys or red hair and freckles and the agrarian state.

Frank smiled over the banister at her and nodded to secure his answer. He welcomed any compliment. But she didn't smile back at him. She had clutched her keys to her chest and looked straight up at him. He waited for a moment to see if the question of nationality would arise. But there was something wrong with her expression. It held more accusation than admiration.

'*Wenn ich diesen Lärm weiter höre, kommt die Polizei.*' The last word was enough. If she heard any more of this noise, she would call the police. The sudden conversion of an admirer into an enemy had left him completely stunned and awkwardly poised on the stairs. His feet, drawn by compliment, were still subconsciously coming back down. Frank said nothing.

'*Sie wohnen bei Evelyn Richter, nicht wahr?*' He wasn't quite sure whether this was meant to confirm that he was living with Evelyn Richter or staying with Evelyn Richter. There was a big difference. Evelyn Richter was the name on his mailbox. That much was right. He was living in her apartment, but in his own separate room. Werner, Evelyn's boyfriend, was living with her.

Frank wasn't about to start explaining anything to the woman with the keys to her chest who had led him into a trap. The glare of her questions over the banisters had registered an insult with him and he turned to continue his climb with redoubled speed.

When Evelyn herself heard about the incident, she created too much of a fuss. At teatime that evening she became very excited.

'*Unglaublich!* It is unbelievable,' she said. She was laying the table at the time. She used wooden boards instead of plates. Her cutlery matched. She placed another board with an assortment of ham, sausage and cheese on the table. She had also chopped some radishes which looked like white coins with red rims. Ten pfennig pieces.

'I will go to this woman and tell her she has nothing to say. She has not the right to say this to you. It is unbelievable.'

Evelyn shook her head. She had straight sandy hair which normally hung to one side. Whenever she looked at someone, she had the habit of slanting her head sideways.

'Wait! I will tell this to Werner when he comes. This woman will hear something from us.'

Frank rarely saw Evelyn's eyes because she wore tinted brown glasses. He was leaning against the radiator with his arms folded. She told him to sit down and placed the earthenware teapot on a candle-lit warmer. Frank asked where Werner was and heard he was visiting his mother. There was a small two-pronged fork lying along the board with the ham. It often looked so decorative that Frank didn't think he should disturb it. He lifted the fork and speared a slice of smoked ham, separating it from the next layer. Evelyn asked him to describe the woman.

'Ach, . . . this is Frau Klempner. We know this woman. She is always looking and talking to the *Hausmeister*.' Evelyn made a duck's beak with her hand to describe.

'Do you know this word, *"plappern"*?'

'It sounds very much like the word prattle in English,' Frank explained, thinking of yet another word, 'babble'. Again, there was a white sheen across Evelyn's glasses. Her mime often explained things much better than her words.

Frank would have ignored the incident or passed it off as one more example of German life to be handed on as a gift or a passing joke to some other fellow musician travelling in Germany. His instinct told him to keep playing his pipes and whistles even louder in spite of this Frau Klempner. But Evelyn made more of it. She treated him as a helpless musician affronted by a typically tyrannical German woman. All art and music had been assaulted by this philistine, Frau Klempner. For Frank, even though it was comforting to be defended by a young woman, the incident was amusing. For Evelyn, it was an attack on freedom. It even infringed her own privacy.

'I don't ask her to close her windows when she's cooking and the stink of onions is everywhere in the courtyard.'

Werner was far more rational. He laughed and said Frau Klempner should be ignored. She had no authority. He seemed tired and sat back in the sofa with his beer. He dismissed the whole thing with a wave of his hand which looked as though he was declining the offer of cake.

'This old one. She has nothing to say.'

Evelyn sat down facing Werner with her knees on the sofa. Her shoes had dropped to the floor. Werner had a layer of froth on his moustache. Evelyn reached over and lifted some of the froth clinging to her finger and put it in her own mouth. Werner then placed his own finger across his moustache and caught the remaining froth with his lower lip.

Three sides of the wide courtyard are covered with windows. The other is a wall clung with scaffolding. Some of the walls between the windows are peeling. Some of the windows have a white sheen across them. The workmen have gone home leaving behind an aftersound of planks and shouts.

Frank saw Evelyn coming across the courtyard in a long coat. He was on his way out while she was coming in. She carried a leather bag which was meant more for documents than for personal things. She looked different. It was the first time he had seen her wearing that coat. It was the first time he had seen her at a distance, walking towards him. She seemed smaller. The new perspective of the open courtyard with its windows and scaffolding made her look compact. He saw her as somebody he didn't know.

The furniture in her apartment makes Evelyn Richter stand out. The immured dimensions of her apartment give an illusion of size. Tables, chairs, sofa, the 18-inch television set alter her shape. The height of the pictures hung in her apartment make her seem more friendly. The poster in the kitchen of the Folies Bergère. The shoes beside the sofa make her younger, more like a child. In the courtyard, she looks smaller, fuller, more official and unknown.

She looks like part of the underground throngs. An individual observed on a crowded train. An unknown person with an imagined unlimited biography. A person in a long beige coat carrying a leather bag. A rather official-looking bag. A person without gender on the way home from work. A person who buys a monthly ticket. A young woman with a public smile for the ticket vendor.

She looks like a person whose mother might own a dachshund or a red setter. A person who has just bought some cheese or unsalted butter at the cheese shop. Who paused briefly before putting her U-Bahn ticket into her bag. Who thought she was being stared at by an elderly man on the U-Bahn. Who avoids making eye contact on the underground trains. Whose view of two children is blocked by someone standing in front of her on the U-Bahn. Who glances at the headlines of the evening paper in someone else's hands and who looks away again because it's unmannerly and would also form an association with the man sitting down with his evening paper. Who holds on firmly to the vertical bar on the U-Bahn whenever she can't get a seat. Who looks at the familiar, numberless clock on her way out of the U-Bahn station. Who held her bag against the counter of the cheese shop with her knee while she took out her purse. Who heard the combined surge of traffic behind her after she had crossed the road. Who had hoped that the green man would stay green a little longer.

A person who has just placed a packet of Danish cheese along with a packet of unsalted butter into a rather official-looking bag. Who passes the wine shop without hesitation. Passes the Eros centre without noticing it. Who has never even been inside a sex shop. Passes a Turkish woman in the street with her child and wonders how a Turkish woman can wear so many layers of clothes, even in spring. Who thinks Turkish children look pretty. Feels a slight dampness under her arms. Thought Danish cheese would be nice for tea. Never eats garlic. Who has never been to South America but would love to go. Who has never been to Ireland but who knows somebody from Ireland. Who has no wish to go to Turkey ever because there are so many Turkish people living in Berlin. Never speaks about school and never associates with any of her old classmates. Who hates a man called Dieter Opp and who hopes she will never see him again. Who is not too keen on her parents coming to visit her in Berlin.

For whom the conglomerate smell of cheeses at the cheese shop becomes too much after a few minutes. Who emerges from the cheese shop and glances right and left looking for inspiration before continuing her journey home. Who loves Greek food and Greek music. Finds Irish music haunting and medieval. Cannot stand eastern music. Who used to like South American music but who has gone off it somewhat lately. Finds Irish people more European than a lot of Italians. Finds unsalted butter much more pleasant than the salted ones. Finds it incomprehensible that her brother would join the army, particularly after what happened to their father during the war. Whose father refuses to speak about the war. Who writes a letter to her brother asking him not to join the army but receives no answer from him.

Has a general phobia about posting letters which causes a moment of fear and irreversible helplessness once the letter disappears. Once had an older man from Charlottenburg for a boyfriend but put an end to it because he began to remind her too much of her father. Who still tends to compare all boyfriends with her father. Who can't help thinking about her own letter at the bottom of the yellow post-box. Who always insists on discussing all her previous affairs and relationships with any new boyfriend and expects them to do the same. Who tends to bite with abject ferocity at that moment when approaching rapture with her lover. Who was warned many times by one man never again to use her teeth but forgets herself sometimes, causing him once to walk out in the middle of the night saying he would never be back, but did return a week later and was no longer welcome. Though he managed to sleep with her once more, she made sure she didn't bite him on that final turn. Who has a steady relationship which has gone on for the past few years with one man. Who is in no rush to have a baby. Who has orgasms. Who does not bite her current boyfriend.

Is in possession of a sad feature in her eyes which illuminates a paternal longing in all men. Whose strange blend of sadness and comical appearance is noticed on the U-Bahn. Whose skin attracts mosquitoes. Whose eyes are normally hidden by her lightly tinted glasses. Who has a slight tendency to put on weight around the thighs and who suppresses this with regular swimming followed by saunas. Whose hand firmly clutches the bar on the U-Bahn between the grip of an older man and that of a younger man. Who doesn't notice the collection of knuckles along the bar. Who is observed in detail by the younger man looking at her knuckles and following her wrist along the sleeve to trace its owner. Whose head is turned away from the young man on the U-Bahn who has been studying her arm, her hair and her knuckles and contemplated pressing on one of her knuckles to make her turn around so that he could see if the face matched what the hair and knuckles promised. Whose face with its sad look does belong to the knuckles along the vertical bar.

Who received an expensive camera once from her current partner in the early days of their relationship and only shot two rolls of colour film on their first holiday after which she abandoned it. Who would very dearly like to gain possession of a particular photograph which was taken years ago on a time release which shows her smiling and clutching a bottle of champagne while being embraced from behind by Dieter Opp with his hand inside her pink knickers and his chin resting on her left shoulder glancing downwards at her naked breasts. Who is known in the cheese shop. Who carries a bag which does not look like it contains anything such as Danish cheese or unsalted butter. Of whom it is often difficult to tell whether she's looking straight ahead or downwards. Who knows what time it is. Whose hand holds the handle of her bag. Who pushes the heavy front door of the house with her shoulder. Who wears a knee-length coat. Whose arms are inside the coat. Whose hair touches the collar of the coat. Whose chin is round. Whose feet touch the ground. Who has eyes. Who can speak. Breathes, hears, sees in front of her. Is an inhabitant of Berlin.

The windows on all three sides look out on to the courtyard. The tenants can all see out on to their courtyard which has a cluster of olive trees along with some flower boxes as its central feature. It is difficult to tell when people are actually looking out on to their courtyard. Some windows are left open. The tenants are discouraged from hanging out washing through the windows.

Evelyn and Frank meet in the courtyard some ten metres away from the centre. They stop and talk for a moment. The courtyard with all its windows forces them to meet as strangers of people who just know each other vaguely. Frank is in a rush and has a box containing his instruments under his arm. With a clenched fist he tries to indicate running or lateness or hurry. Evelyn has stopped and is holding her bag with both hands. Frank tries to leave on a humorous note.

'What have you done to Frau Klempner? I haven't seen her in weeks. Have you done away with her?'

Evelyn smiles and shakes her head.

'Nothing! I leave her alone.' Evelyn has transferred her bag to the left hand.

The phone rang in the room, suspending his playing in mid-reel. There did follow just two more notes but they had already lost power. The instrument had been winded. The drones lost their momentum and expired. Even the invisible beat was overpowered by the new beat of the phone.

He placed his hand, holding the chanter, under the drones and walked over to the phone in a stoop. Placing one thigh and buttock on the armrest of the sofa, he cradled the pipes in his lap with his arm. The other leg, bound around the thigh with a leather piece like an eye-patch, was poised for balance, knee bent, ready to raise him up again. The green velvet bag with its meretricious tassels, exhaled with a final sigh of unmusical breath. He crouched over the table and picked up the white receiver.

'*Bei Richter*,' he answered. It was Werner. He spoke in a calm, unhurried English. It was unusual to talk to Werner on the phone and Frank had to visualize his moustache before he could speak. He wondered if Werner had left something behind. But Werner was very conversational. Frank explained that he was keeping the evil spirit of Frau Klempner away with the sound of his uillean pipes.

'You have no concert tonight?' Werner asked. It amused Frank that all performances, even though most of his took place in small pubs, were referred to as concerts. He had taught Evelyn to call them 'gigs'.

'No, there's nothing on tonight. No concert.'

'Frank . . . if you have no plans tonight, we could meet us somewhere. I have something to discuss with you. Can we meet us in the restaurant Zum Römer. You know this one?'

Frank agreed and asked what they were going to discuss.

'We will talk about this at dinner, Zum Römer. Can we say eight o'clock?'

Frank closed his eyes and began to play again but he couldn't regain the drive of the music. He couldn't concentrate. It wasn't the first time Werner had formally announced that he was going to discuss something. Usually it was quite straightforward. The first thing was the matter of phone calls. Werner had asked him instead of leaving money beside the phone, to record them all in a booklet beside the phone which they could add up at the end of the month. Then there was the matter of a token rent for the room. Then there was the business of the cheese. This had been split into two issues. The fact that it was unfair to take the last piece of cheese without replacing it with more. Cheese was there to be eaten but only on condition that successors were provided for as well. The other issue concerned the way the cheese was cut, which was also with successors in mind. Cheese should not be approached from all sides at once and should never be cut between knife and thumb. They had many discussions which often spilled over into broader issues, preoccupied mainly with the difference between Germany and Ireland. Only once had the discussion gone too far when Frank had said: 'The only thing wrong with Germany is that it's not surrounded by water.' All other occasions had been more than friendly and disciplined.

When Frank arrived at the restaurant, Werner and Evelyn were already sitting at a table. He was surprised to see Evelyn there. He was also surprised to see that the Römer was otherwise empty. His memory of the Römer was that of a crowded restaurant. It was early. Frank made his way over to them as directly as possible. At one stage, he was forced to walk sideways between two chairs but keeping his destination in sight. He could have carried on along the wall behind Evelyn and Werner which showed the blanched sunlit steps leading down into the warm olive-lined streetscape of southern Italy. Werner shook hands.

'I have ordered a pizza for myself. You should have one too and a nice beer.' The waiter, having stalked Frank's diagonal progress across the restaurant, timed the moment with the sliding menu. At the same time, Evelyn raised her glass of red wine to her lips. Things were unusually formal. A decision was made and the waiter left, coming back moments later with a beer for Frank.

'The pizza here is the best in all Berlin,' Werner said. 'Nearly as good as in Italy.'

'Well, I've never been to Italy so I couldn't comment.'

'Ah, you must go! Evelyn and I, we have been in Italy three times since we met. It is very expensive but we like it very much.' Frank's eyes travelled from Werner to Evelyn and then on to the beer in front of him and in another circle back to Werner and then on to Evelyn again who was nodding in agreement.

'Of course. Italy is the best country for holidays,' she said.

Werner's pizza arrived followed shortly by Frank's pizza. The waiter had brought an extra plate for Evelyn who said she could only manage a small corner. As Werner began to cut a triangular slice, she repeated; not so much, not so much. Frank suggested it might be easier to cut a pizza with a pair of scissors. They laughed. It allowed Frank to slow down the circle which his eyes made around the table from Werner over to Evelyn and down to his own beer and on to Werner's pizza and Werner himself and back to Evelyn who was sitting up with her back straight, looking down at the geometric slice on the plate in front of her. Frank's own pizza gave him something to concentrate on. Werner's moustache appeared to be damp and curled into his mouth at one point. Evelyn cut a small triangle from the big triangle and raised it to her mouth on a fork.

It doesn't take long to eat a pizza. The only things left on Frank's plate are two olive stones. On Werner's, the stems of three chilli peppers. Beyond Evelyn, on the wall, there is a pillar beyond which there is a woman bearing an urn on her way down to a hot plaza. Frank's beer is half full. Werner leans back in his chair and dusts off any possible crumbs from his trousers with his hand.

'Frank, . . . I think you are waiting for me to discuss this with you now. It is something very important to me and to Evelyn also. For two weeks now, I have been thinking. In the beginning I thought it was only in my mind, but now I think I am right. I think Evelyn is falling in love with you.'

With thumb and forefinger, Werner parts his moustache to each side. Frank looks at Evelyn who has her elbows on the table. Her hair has partly fallen over her face. He looks at the ashtray on the table and then back to Werner.

'I have spoken to Evelyn about this. It is true. She has also agreed that something is happening to her. Frank, . . . I don't want to make an accusation against you. I am not angry with you. But I think I must talk to you about this openly.'

Werner continues to explain. It has caught Frank like a

compliment which he cannot instinctively deny. He could say nothing.

'I think about this every day now. All the time I think it is going to end with me and Evelyn. I think she will be in love with you very soon. I cannot stop it and I must talk to you before this happens.'

Evelyn has said nothing either. It looks almost as if she is incapable of acting involuntarily. Unharnessed. Why could she not just speak for herself? Frank's first impulse was to turn to Evelyn and ask her directly whether this was true. But her silence had already admitted it. Frank had to say something. At the same time, he didn't want to insult Evelyn by renouncing interest.

'Werner, I must say, this is a total surprise to me. I can tell you honestly, this is the first time anything of the sort entered my head.' It was too much of a defence.

'But I am not accusing you, Frank. I will not make you feel like a criminal that has betrayed me. I like you. I want to be your friend. But I think something is going to happen between Evelyn and you and this would make me very sad.'

Frank tries to assure Werner that there is no intentional threat on his side. He cannot speak for Evelyn. Evelyn is still looking at the table in front of her.

'Don't worry, Werner. I have no intention of causing any trouble like that.' Frank wonders what effect this has on Evelyn. Werner continues.

'You see, Evelyn and I, we love each other very much. We never talk about the future but we are very much in love. If this comes to an end, I cannot stop it . . . All the time, I think this will happen. I think it is going to end with us. Evelyn and I have talked about this. She has said you are very attractive. You are very sympathetic. I think this myself. You are a good friend . . . But for Evelyn, I think you are also attractive in a sexual way. I know this is very natural and I cannot stop it. But this will be a tragedy for me.'

Frank's gaze resumes its lap of the table from Werner around

The Compound Assembly of E. Richter

to Evelyn in the hope that she will say something. When she remains silent he brings his eyes down to his glass which is now almost empty. The more she continues to be silent, the more he is compelled to dissociate himself from her. But he doesn't want to dissociate himself.

Evelyn has not looked at Frank. Frank cannot look at Evelyn for too long because it would implicate him. Her silence makes him an accomplice. Frank cannot look at his beer for too long because it would confirm a plot. He cannot speak directly to Evelyn because it might be seen as collusion. Anything, even a sideways glance between them, would confirm an ongoing conversation. Frank cannot look at Werner for too long without saying something to deny it. He cannot deny it because he cannot speak for Evelyn. He cannot speak for Evelyn if she hasn't told him what's on her mind. He cannot look at the woman with the urn for too long because it might signify disinterest. He cannot speak to Evelyn with Werner at the table. He cannot speak to Werner without talking about Evelyn.

Frank must find a way to talk to Evelyn through Werner. Or to Werner through Evelyn. He could talk to his beer with both of them.

'Look, Werner, I will tell you the truth. Evelyn happens to be one of the most beautiful women that I have ever met. I can say that unreservedly. I think you're very lucky. But Evelyn is also a good friend. And so are you. I like Evelyn very much, but that's where it stays. I couldn't possibly imagine anything further happening between us.'

Frank wonders if he is expected to offer to move out of the apartment. But this would also signify admission. He hasn't said enough. But the more he says the more he will admit duplicity. He will soon touch on the ultimate truth that he can imagine anything. Frank is not bereft of desire. He cannot play the eunuch.

Evelyn is playing with a cardboard match which she has torn from the gratis matches; *'Zum Römer, Italianische gerichte'*. Is she trying to tie a knot with the match? She must know that people can see the shape of her breasts through the jumper. Frank's eyes are trespassing. He is caught red-handed. He can only imagine being caught. Imagine being caught coming out of the Eros shop just at that moment when Evelyn is passing by. Imagine being caught in Werner and Evelyn's bedroom. He remembers being caught in an orchard; while he was hiding behind a hedge, the owner was standing right behind him.

Nothing has changed. Except that the restaurant has become more populated now. The more they sit there, the more the real possibilities become extant in their expressions. The more they discuss it the more it becomes true. Frank must take on Evelyn's silence. He must find out whether she is just enjoying a compliment or whether she really has something for him. Frank must speak to Werner on Evelyn's behalf. Perhaps a double negative somewhere might stir the veracity of her silence.

'Listen, Werner,' Frank knows how to look earnest. 'You have absolutely nothing to worry about. You don't have to worry about me and you certainly don't have to worry about Evelyn either. She may have a passing attraction for me, though I haven't noticed. But she really loves you. Anyone can see that. If she was in any way interested in me, we wouldn't be sitting around the table here. It would have been out in the open long ago. She would have said something. I definitely think it's all your imagination, Werner.'

Frank is talking for Evelyn as if she has no mind. He becomes her mouthpiece. Frank can say what she wants to say. He can make her say what she doesn't want to say. He can make her say what Werner wants to hear. He can make her say what he himself wants to hear. He can say what she never intended to say. He can make her say what she wants Werner to hear. He could make her say what she wants to say but doesn't want Werner to hear. He can say what she wants Frank to hear. He can also make her say what she doesn't want to hear herself say. He can provoke her. As long as she says nothing herself, she assents.

'Total fantasy! Any attraction that Evelyn has for me is entirely her love for Irish music. She also likes to speak English. Like everyone else, Evelyn enjoys the company of a foreigner. She loves the music and is fascinated by the way musicians live. In that way, I represent something new. Something carefree maybe. But Evelyn has much more definite views about men. I don't fit into her scheme and never would either. I'm not even her type of man. Evelyn thinks I'm too skinny. I'm too unhealthy. Evelyn would say I'm too much of a man's man. She thinks I'm too much in love with beer and music and good crack. I wouldn't be her sort in a million years.'

The sight of his empty glass between his hands gives Frank the first chance to move outside the circle. He holds his glass up in the air and looks towards the bar. A fishing net hangs over the bar, floating aloft with bottle-green buoys, illuminated with blue-green nautical lights from the midnight Adriatic.

It was almost noon when Evelyn got up. She opened the window and let in the wet, gritty sounds of cement and plastering. It came in repeated sounds of slapping cement. Shovels turning moist cement piles with a sideways slice. A repeated dash of cement against the wall followed by semicircular or circular sounds of levelling. Trowels scooped matter from mortar boards.

Evelyn's breasts rippled like fine plaster. Her hair fell to one side like sand. She turned away from the window and her thighs and bottom shimmered with movement. With one leg already in her trousers, she had to hop on that foot to get into the other side. The skin beneath her white knickers was somewhere between powder and liquid. Somewhere between solid state and fluid, held together by surface tension. As soon as she pulled her trousers up, it became more solid. Her back bent forward as she stepped into her shoes. It looked matt varnished. A light blue jumper hid the remaining skin from the warm daylight. Evelyn first put on her glasses before she turned to speak in a soft, semi-fluid voice. She left behind a cool metallic taste.

Above and Beyond

I wasn't able to talk that day. But I had my fists sunk deep into my coat. It's always that way. Whenever I see people, I can say nothing. And the street was fast and full of people. And she was beside me. So I couldn't find anything to say. But it was a good day for us. We were in the city and she had money. And she was as slow as I was. It was cold. Only cold outside. Her knuckles were crushed and red and half-hidden by the sleeves of her coat. Even though I said nothing, she looked at me again. I don't know if I was smiling because we looked down and saw money falling in the street. All coins rolling away in semicircles. I know the sound of coins very well. And I saw her crushed hands coming up from her pockets. I thought it was water but it was money, more money. I looked at her eyes and I couldn't say anything and I couldn't stop her throwing money down, so I walked away. But she followed me and I stopped. I couldn't hit her so she walked into the shop where I saw her pushing one of the people and spilling more money on the floor. Then she followed me again and tried to kick me because her knuckles were crushed and her face was red. But she couldn't get me because she fell down in the street and I couldn't kick her because it was too late and a guard had picked her up by the neck. So she started screaming and trying to hit me again and the people stopped to look, so there was nothing I could say. And she tried to hit the guard and kept on screaming because she has a voice. I don't. I only say what I hear. When I hear somebody say something, I think I've said it myself. And I heard somebody say the guard was going to take her away.

Above and Beyond

A crowd has gathered at the end of Talbot Street. They have no time to stop but the sight of people gathered looking in one direction compels them to look. Nothing better to do than to see what others are looking at. A guard with black leather gloves is holding a girl, a traveller girl, by the collar. He is tall, which makes it look as though her feet don't touch the ground. Her movements lack balance or skill, like an infant. Her whine for liberty is half-directed at the crowd, staging pain and brutality. Perhaps their spectator stares might force him to set her free. Her partner stands by, silent, watching her scream.

'Lemme go – lemme go.'

There is something in her hand which she pushes up towards the guard.

'Have a sniff a that. Go on, why don't ye? Have a sniff.'

Her voice is hoarse like a cat under a caravan. Her teeth sound numb with saliva. She coughs her damp lungs to make him let her go. But he tells her to keep quiet, looking down at her like a flight of concrete steps. The people of Dublin speak like rain.

She's very young. She could be only sixteen. What did she do? She must-a done something. Look at her, she can't stand. Your man is no better. I seen her in the shop over there. I seen her pushing a lady. He's got an awful lot of patience with her. I would-a given her a box. I say I'd give her a box in the ear.

She's only young. Would you look at your man? He's footless. It's a rough life, poor thing. She's only about sixteen. Ah, she has it coming.

The guard's collar is tight with authority. His hand is inside a black glove. His head is under a hat. The street is underfoot. Music comes out from the shops. Bargains face out on the street. The man's eyes are facing out. Onlookers face in towards the girl in the grip of a guard. A crowd of people knows something. They know she's very young. They know where the bargains are. They know what it's like to put on a new coat. What it's like to put on the old one again. What it's like to be inside a coat. Inside shoes. Under a hat. In a street. On your own. In a crowd. In front of food. Outside music. Under illusion. Inside the law. In front of

TVs. Behind husbands. Beside girlfriends. Beyond help. Overlooked. Underestimated. Well informed. Left of centre. Ill-defined. Self-contained. Unattached. Round-shouldered. Sympathetic.

Some of them speak with pity. Some of them know better.

'Ah, they're just awful, them two. I seen her in the shop over there.'

They look at the guard whose breath touches the girl's head. She tries again to get away. She reminds everyone of the cold. She reminds everyone of their own homes.

A crowd forms of the longing to remain separate. People speak to each other to keep their distance. People are tall because others are small. They gather and divide into a crowd of individuals. They collate and stand looking so as not to be looked at. So as not to be recognized. Fame is the most excessive form of anonymity. And success is pure failure. They watch somebody being arrested for a sense of dignity. People keep budgies to remind themselves of freedom. People keep children so they can forget about themselves. A man joins the crowd so nobody will know he's just got a haircut. A woman in the crowd speaks her mind to let everyone know she's part of the crowd. Another woman adjusts her underwear so that nobody will notice her. Women wear lipstick so people can't see them. You need a crowd so you can look for yourself. You need music so you can hear yourself. You wear shoes so you can stand up. You get on a bus so you can look out. You eat to prove you're alive. You speak to find out what you're on about. You tell people about yourself because you want to know about them. You admit your mistake so you can go on making mistakes in greater comfort. People stand in the street so that seagulls can fly overhead. You kick a dog so you can feel your foot. You stroke a dog so you can feel your foot another time. You walk the dog because you're afraid of yourself. You eat a sandwich to find out if you're hungry. Pubs are there to keep people away from each other. Shops are there for people to walk past each other. The owner of a shop belongs to his customers. The owner of a car belongs to his car. The man who beats his wife is at her mercy.

While the river stands still, the city moves on. While some let go, others hold on. While a guard holds out his arm for the crowd, a girl dances beneath his breath. While a woman looks in her bag, a man beside her looks away. While a girl dances, a woman asks her husband for money. You watch the girl while you stand in a crowd. You read a book to confirm that you're not the only one. While you read a book, a couple make love. While people kiss, the city stands still. While Matt Talbot kneels down, a woman gets up to put on her sock. While you turn your back on the girl, it takes place right in front of your eyes. While more people talk, less is being said. While agreements are signed, the sheets are being stained. Ireland unstained shall never be at peace. While somebody looks up, somebody else flinches in sunlight. While somebody remembers his ancestors, a woman's nostrils expand with the smell. While you might be lucky to be alive, you might be unlucky enough to be a republican. While some are afflicted with a good education, some are better off joining the guards. People stand in the street because they feel more at home. The woman whose home is decorated with hundreds of ornaments, brass ornaments, clocks, commemoration plaques, coats of arms, a bull brought back from Spain, a porcelain grotto from Lourdes, a picture of John F. Kennedy and Pope John, a copper sailing boat and a silver-plated shoe, can easily get lost among the crowd. The woman who owns a porcelain grotto will see porcelain grottoes all over Dublin. A woman with red shoes will see other women with red shoes. While you might want to be like your friends, everything you own will betray you. Clothes are worn so you can tell people apart. Pubs are there to keep friends apart. You hit somebody so you can get to know them better. You get on better with those you dislike. A cavalry of traffic awaits the instruction to charge while a woman lifts her foot from the pavement. Thomas Moore is on the point of speaking while somebody shoves a tenner in his back pocket. While a woman looks down at her shoes, people keep looking up to politicians. A man with his hand in his pocket disappears into government buildings while pupils with ink on their hands emerge from school with pop idols inscribed on their schoolbags. A hand makes gradual progress underneath a schoolgirl's jumper in the lane by Granby's, while onions are being sliced in Chinese restaurants. People think of the approaching evening as others remember the morning falling away. As a girl shouts under the grip of a guard, people gather to hide their own feelings. A man stands mute and inert, watching his girl in the grip of a guard. A blue car arrives with blue flashing light, while somewhere else a man sits down, places his elbows on the table and prepares to take the first bite from a hamburger held up at eye level. A woman in the crowd says, 'But she's so young.' Another woman says, 'They're taking her away.'

The man is unable to say a word because someone in the crowd has already said it. What he wants to say is being said by the crowd. Slowly, he points to the girl's head and on realizing this, she pulls back her hair to uncover an old gash in her skull. The people in the crowd instantly whisper and forget their own pain. While two more guards step from the blue car, the first guard breathes on the girl and a woman in the crowd says, 'I don't know.' While nobody knows why she's being taken away, somebody says, 'She must have done something.' While her friend can say nothing, somebody says, 'They're taking her in the car.' And while the man cannot stop her going, somebody says, 'Where are they taking her?' As she resists, holding on to the door of the blue car, somebody says, 'Look, she's not going.' And as the man watches her resisting, the people of Dublin speak like rain. Then she turns to the crowd and shouts, 'What are ye all looking at?' and repeats with screaming dignity, 'What are ye looking at, ye?' and the people in the crowd suddenly begin to move without actually going anywhere. And they continue to move as the girl shouts back at them again, 'Go on, look at ye.' As another guard helps to force her into the car, she turns to him and says, 'Take a sniff a that.' And while the crowd begins to laugh, the guards become impatient. A fist strikes her in the ribs as her partner stands motionless in the street, now almost becoming part of the crowd watching her while somebody says, 'Ah, there's no need for that.' And others quietly repeat, 'There's no need for that. She far too young.' Now he sees her through the windows sitting in the back seat of the blue car. She's being taken away for the sake of the crowd. She sits in the back seat to remind everyone that they're standing in the street. Then she begins to beat her fists down on the necks of the two guards sitting in the front seats and the crowd begins to laugh again while the man stands mute and the crowd says, 'Look she's hittin' the two in front. Would you look at her.' Now the crowd almost becomes proud of her. She's one of their own. And the first guard gets into the back seat beside her and places the fist within its black glove in her ribs, while somebody says, 'There's no need for that.' And the blue car pulls away while her partner is left behind. As the people disperse, he remains in that spot. While the people stop talking, he stops saying anything, and his fists are sunk deep in his coat.